I0638624

SWEDISH PORTRAITS

Five Short Stories

By
Judit Martin

About the Author

Judit Martin grew up in the American Midwest and received her BA in English and history from Washington State University in 1961. After teaching for several years, she moved to Europe to travel, eventually settling in Sweden in 1969. She lives in an old house in the countryside near the mining village of Zinkgruvan and worked for many years as a weather observer for the Swedish weather bureau.

She has published several short stories in Scottish literary magazines and two books in Swedish: one about people who have been weather observers, and the other about daily life in the mining village at the beginning of the last century. *Augusta's Daughter,* her first novel published in English and released in 2012, is about life in nineteenth century Sweden.

Author's Note: This book is a work of fiction. Any resemblance to actual places, events, or persons living or dead is purely coincidental.

Photo front cover: Adolfslund, Zinkgruvan, Sweden, originally the home of a family with eleven children.

Graphic Design: Esther Feske

Editors: Mary Sharp, Whitney Pope, Deb Schense, and Joan Liffring-Zug Bourret

ISBN-10: 1932043888
ISBN-13: 978-1932043884

Library of Congress Control Number: 2012955617
©2012 Copyright Judit Martin
Printed in the U.S.A

Contents

INTRODUCTION TO FIVE SHORT STORIES

Up until the middle of the 1950s, life for those living in the Swedish countryside was much the same as it had been for centuries. Not only did the poor live under primitive material conditions, but their treatment, by those considered to be their superiors, was often inhumane—especially when it came to children, who were merely looked upon as a source of free labor and incapable of having feelings. But life had always been so and few had higher expectations. They made the most of the situations in which they found themselves. Four of these stories are inspired by the lives of people I have known, or known about, who lived under the shadow of their superiors.

The story of Alulf, on the other hand, is completely fictional. He was originally inspired by a picture of a man lying on his bed looking at the photos on his wall, and once I had created him I had no idea where he was going. I simply watched his life unfold as my pen moved across the paper, often finding myself curious or surprised by his actions. Such is the fun of writing!

SAMUEL

Holding the edges of her heavy shawl together with one hand and clutching the letter in her other hand, Emma plowed her way up the snow-covered hill from the village, driven by her excitement. At last! Impatiently she kicked the snow off her high-buttoned boots and, without bothering to shake off the hem of her ankle-length skirt, rushed into the house.

"Papa!" she shouted at the top of her voice, disregarding the families in the two downstairs flats as she hurried up the stairs noisily. "Papa has a letter from America!"

Samuel looked up from where he sat tailor-fashion on his cutting table, surrounded by pins and needles, scissors, tissue paper pattern pieces, and scraps of cloth. Although he was just over fifty, his full beard was pure white. Otherwise his body gave no indication of his age, aside from a few tiny crows' feet fanning out from the corners of his somewhat sad blue eyes.

He took the letter, turning it over slowly. It bore no return address, only a black postmark stamped across George Washington's face. Squinting, he could barely make out the words "Groton, S. D. Nov. 16, 1909." The handwriting below was definitely Walter's. Like others of his generation, Samuel was not a man to show emotion. But his shaking hand betrayed him. It had been over a year since he had heard from his only son, and he had begun to fear the worst. It was not uncommon that young men who went to America "to seek their fortune" were seemingly swallowed up by that huge continent and never heard of again. Seeing Walter's handwriting now was as if he had suddenly come home again. Emma backed out of the room and closed the door quietly, leaving her father alone with Walter's long-awaited letter.

Samuel cleared a pathway across the cutting table and dropped nimbly to the floor. In the desk drawer among buttons and spools of thread, he found the letter-opener that had once belonged to his father. Sliding its ivory tip under the corner of the flap, he slit open the envelope. Carefully he pulled out the single sheet of paper, unfolded it, and smoothed the creases against the table top. It was written in pencil, with the last sentences trailing like ivy around the edges of the page. After some searching through the tangle of words, he finally found the beginning.

"Beloved Father," it began. "God's peace and grace be with thee. I hope this letter finds thee in good health. I apologize for my long silence. I have just returned from many months of prospecting out west in Indian Territory. I was shot in the leg during a raid and lay for weeks in a make-shift hospital, but now I am finally back home in South Dakota. I was greatly shocked and saddened to hear of Mother's death. I had no idea she was ill. I understand that Father is going to be very lonely without her, especially once Emma is married. Could he think to come and live with me in America? I am in the process of obtaining a small farm under the Homestead Act. I can receive the land for free as long as I build a house and farm it. It would be nice to have a little company..."

Samuel let the letter fall to the table without reading further. Unlike his daughters, who were occupied with their husbands, children, and homes in Chicago, Walter was alone and understood loneliness. His words touched him in a place he had avoided going to since his wife's death. True, Emma was still at home. She was only seventeen, but already engaged. He couldn't bring himself to ask her to give up her future with Fritz and stay home to become a traditional *"hemma dotter"* in order to care for him for the rest of his life. Nor could he imagine re-marrying and sharing his life with another woman. At the same time, he couldn't help wondering how he would manage once Emma moved away. It was she who cooked and cleaned and washed his clothes. Men did not do such work; they didn't even know how. Of course, many widowers or unmarried men had housekeepers, but all too often such situations became complicated, resulting in illegitimate children and sometimes forced marriages. But most of all, he missed not having Matilda close by, for he had grown very fond of her.

Samuel sat down by the window and gazed out at the snow-covered forest, remembering when he and Matilda had met in a neighboring village over a quarter of a century earlier...

...The day was sunny and warm, even though it was the middle of October. Golden birch leaves dotted the path through the forest, while the last yellowing aspen leaves twisted on their stems, seemingly anxious to detach themselves and experience the once-in-a-lifetime free fall to the ground below. Samuel and his father, Torbjörn, better known as Tailor-Tor, were making their annual round through the parish, measuring, cutting, and sewing winter clothes for the members of each household. Because most country folk wore the same clothes day after day, they needed to be replaced at least once a year. As was the custom, the local tailor lived with each family while he sewed for them, enabling him to make the necessary fittings and adjustments as he worked.

After having spent several weeks sewing in poor peasant homes, where the fare was the usual porridge, "blue" milk, salted herring, and potatoes, and the mattresses were bags filled with straw, they were now on their way to the richest estate in the parish. Samuel had passed it many times, but he had never been through the gates. As a child, he had been afraid to go near the place, for it was rumored that anyone caught trespassing was beaten. Even now that he was an adult, having been confirmed in the state church when he had turned thirteen, he felt uneasy following his father through the gate and along the gravel driveway to the side door.

"I'm tailor Nordström and this is my son, Samuel," his father told the maid who opened the door.

"Madame Sahlin is waiting in the drawing room," they were told. "Follow me."

She led them along a hall and opened the door to a large room filled with heavy furniture. A middle-aged woman was sitting beside a round table, a coffee cup in her hand.

"I have been awaiting Nordström since yesterday," she remarked coldly as soon as the door was closed behind them.

"My humble apologies," Torbjörn answered, bowing. "It is not always possible to know ahead of time how long a job will take."

"It can't take so much time to throw together something for those good-for-nothings in the shacks down the road," she snorted.

As much as Torbjörn detested the attitude of the rich toward the poor, who were poor because the rich refused to pay them decent wages, he looked at the floor and said nothing. Sewing for the people on the estate, was his biggest job and he couldn't afford to lose it.

"Next time Nordström will start his rounds here at the estate," she told him.

"Yes, Madame," Torbjörn replied simply.

It took them several weeks to cut and sew for the Sahlins and their hired help. Each person was called in individually and measured for whichever piece of clothing they were to have made. For the farmhands, it was a question of a shirt or a pair of pants, which were a portion of their yearly pay. For the housemaids it was a matter of a blouse or a skirt. (A new apron was an extra bonus.) They started with the squire and his wife and children, all of whom required everything from church clothes to everyday clothes to outdoor clothes. The ordinary peasants, on the other hand, made most of their own clothes themselves.

One day when Samuel had gone out to relieve himself behind the woodshed, he heard laughter coming from the barn. Suddenly, the heavy door swung open, and one of the milkmaids ran out across the yard toward him, crying. Nervously, he stepped closer to the building and finished his business. But she ran past without seeing him and disappeared into the washhouse, slamming the door behind her. The next day he once again saw her run crying from the barn, followed by the same jeering laughter. Yet another day he saw her pick up a small child who had stumbled and fallen. He could hear her soothing cooing as she cradled it in her arms, until one of the housemaids came running across the yard toward her waving a stick.

"Put that child down, you slut! How many times have you been told not to touch the children. We don't want them covered with lice!"

The milkmaid set the child on the ground gently just as the stick struck the back of her legs. She winced involuntarily.

"Who is that?" Samuel asked a farmhand who had also witnessed the incident.

The young man looked at him incredulously.

"Has Samuel never heard of Crazy-Matilda?"

"Yes, of course, I have but..."

"That's her who runs from the barn and gives people lice." He wrinkled his nose in disgust.

"But what's wrong with her?"

"She's a bastard. Her mother was a bastard, too. She lay in the hay with any man who wanted her. And Matilda is the same."

"How does one know that?"

"Because she has a bastard daughter."

"Does she still lie with men?" Samuel wondered.

"Once a whore, always a whore. Samuel can try her himself."

The thought disgusted him. He had been brought up in a God-fearing family, where men only lay with their wives, and that only for the purpose of procreation.

"But why is she called Crazy Matilda?"

"Because she's stupid. She can't read or write and she can barely count. She has to make a chalk mark on the wall for every liter of milk the cows give."

"But that doesn't make her crazy," Samuel persisted.

"See for yourself. Go and talk to her."

That evening after supper, Samuel waited outside for Matilda to finish eating. She never ate with the others. Instead, she was made to wait until everyone had finished, whereupon she sat alone in a corner of the kitchen and ate leftover scraps from a bowl. She hesitated when she came out onto the porch and saw him waiting.

"Hello," he said. "I'm Nordström's son, Samuel."

"What does Herr Nordström want with me?" she asked with a sigh of resignation.

"I wondered if I may walk a little ways with Matilda."

"Just like all the others," she remarked sarcastically.

"What does Matilda mean?"

"Men are all the same. They get me by myself and force themselves on me, then say that I am a whore."

"I am not like the others," he answered her. "I want nothing from Matilda, I promise. Just to walk and chat with her."

"People will make fun of Herr Nordström—or worse—if they see him with me," she warned.

"Let them," he declared, walking beside her.

"But why does Herr Nordström want to walk with me?" she asked.

Samuel thought for a moment, unsure as to what his motive had actually been.

"I don't think anyone should be treated the way Matilda is treated by people here," he said finally.

She shrugged. "I'm used to it. It began when I was born. My mother was treated the same way. It is the fate of people like us."

They continued walking for a while. Samuel was at a loss for what to say.

"Matilda hasn't been measured for her new clothes," he remarked finally, glancing at her ragged blouse and patched skirt.

"I'm not to get new clothes," she said simply.

"But why not?"

"They say I don't need them because no one ever sees me."

"Is that really true?"

"Yes, it is so."

Samuel had often heard rumors about how badly the Sahlins treated those who worked for them, but he had always assumed such tales were exaggerated. But obviously not.

By now they had reached the barn.

"I must go in and clean up behind the cows before the foreman comes and beats me for laziness," she told him.

Samuel gasped. "Maybe we can talk another day then," he offered.

"Maybe."

Matilda filled his thoughts for the rest of the evening. In spite of the harshness of her life, she seemed to be rather light-hearted. And he had been deeply touched by the way she had picked up the crying child and comforted it, even though she knew she would be punished for doing so.

During their few remaining days on the Sahlin's estate, he went out of his way to cross paths with Matilda. There was a goodness about her that attracted him. A motherliness. Whether the attraction was for the person she was or out of pity was not something he troubled himself over. Quite simply, he liked to be with her, and he felt he could give her a better life than what she had hitherto experienced.

When he mentioned this to his father, Torbjörn was taken aback.

"My son, she is ten years older than you. And she has an illegitimate child, not to mention a reputation."

"Her reputation is put on her by the men who use her against her will," Samuel replied. "She is treated worse than an animal here."

Torbjörn was silent for a minute, considering the situation.

"Perhaps you are right. I, too, have seen that she is ill-treated. But remember, marriage is a lifelong commitment. At the same time, if you are going to begin sewing on your own, you are going to need a wife to take care of the household tasks. What does Matilda think about it?"

"I don't know. I haven't asked her yet. But under the circumstances, she can hardly refuse."

Torbjörn patted him on the shoulder.

"True. You have my blessing, my son."

Samuel continued to seek out Matilda as discreetly as possible. But the evening before they were to leave the estate, he approached her more openly.

"Can we go for a walk?" he asked straight out.

"Of course."

They walked along the road a few minutes without speaking.

"I understand that the Nordströms are finished here and will be leaving tomorrow," she remarked finally, to break the silence. There was an unmistakable sadness in her voice. "It has been pleasant to talk together."

"Yes, I think so, too," he replied.

"Perhaps we can talk again next time Herr Nordström comes," she suggested.

"I'm not coming again," he told her. "I'm going to begin sewing on my own this winter."

"Oh," she replied simply.

"But I have a little problem. I am going to need someone to keep house for me while I work and earn money."

Matilda stopped and looked at him.

"They say that I am a good worker," she offered. "Soon it is free week. Maybe I could stop working for the Sahlins and work for Herr Engtröm instead."

"That isn't what I had in mind. I would like Matilda to marry me and we could have a family."

"But Herr Nordström cannot marry me!" she cried. "I am too old. Besides, he certainly has heard that I have a fatherless daughter who lives with my sister. He knows what people say about me."

"None of that matters. I have seen that Matilda is hard-working and kind. I don't want a paid housekeeper. I want a wife."

Matilda shook her head.

"What will people say?"

"They can say what they want. I have a place to live in another village where people don't know either of us. Come with me as my wife."

"But what about my daughter?"

"I can be a father to her."

Matilda left the Sahlins during the free week at the end of October when all farm workers had the right to seek new employment elsewhere if they wished. Madame Sahlin protested her decision, maintaining that Matilda belonged to the estate, since she had no family.

"She is not entitled to move during free week because she is not considered to be hired help, since we don't pay her," she declared, realizing too late what she had said. And thus Matilda was free to marry Samuel.

They made their home outside a nearby village, where they rented the upstairs in a three-family house. Like in other working-class families, the kitchen was the focal point, where they ate, slept, and spent their time. But unlike other working-class families, the other room was not kept as a "best room" for special occasions. Instead, Samuel set up his cutting and sewing table, an ironing board, and his treddle Singer there. A desk served as his office, and a large cupboard held bolts of cloth.

At first Matilda's ten-year-old daughter, Marie, lived with them. But with the arrival of her half sister, she begged to go back to living with her aunt and uncle, where she was the only child.

Matilda was deeply grateful to Samuel for having seen beyond her reputation and given her a new life. Even though she never managed to learn to read or write, she did everything within her power to show Samuel that he had not made a mistake by marrying her. She bore him two daughters and a son during their first six years of marriage, followed five years later by another daughter when she was forty-two. And five years later, at the age of forty-seven, she gave birth to Emma.

Unfortunately, her illiteracy had prevented her from being confirmed, yet Matilda was deeply religious in her own way. She went to church to listen to the music, finding the sermons boring. She believed that all one needed to do to be a good Christian was to live according to the Golden Rule. That single directive made all the rest of Christianity, including the Ten Commandments, and even the Bible itself, redundant. Such views she kept to herself, however, only hinting of them now and then to Samuel. And true to her beliefs, she did her best to do unto others as she would have them do unto her. She kept their home neat and clean, was economical, a loving mother, a true companion to Samuel, and was known in the community for her kindness.

Although Samuel found it difficult to put his emotions into words, he went out of his way to show Matilda how much she meant to him. In his spare time, he sewed clothes for her from his nicest cloth, adding bits of lace he had saved for the collars. During the summer, small bouquets of wildflowers appeared on the kitchen table. He borrowed books he thought she might enjoy from one of his well-to-do customers and read aloud to her on winter evenings while she knitted or mended clothes. And while he welcomed the birth of each new child, they were all secondary to Matilda. A few days after each birth, when she was safely out of danger, he held her hand and silently thanked God for having watched over her.

There were other signals of love that passed between them, unreadable to outsiders: A light touch when they moved around each other in the crowded kitchen, her small tug at his tie to straighten it before he went out, a look. And every night, unbeknownst to each other, they each thanked God for having let their paths cross that day long ago.

The children grew up without any serious illnesses or mishaps. One by one they immigrated to America in search of better economic possibilities, for at that time Sweden had nothing to offer people of their class. Both Samuel and Matilda were filled with sorrow each time one of them left, uncertain as to whether they would ever see them again. At the same time, they looked forward to growing old together, just the two of them. At last, only Emma was still at home. She was seventeen and engaged to Fritz, a young man in the next village.

One Saturday afternoon when Samuel had taken a pause from his work and went into the kitchen to see if there was any coffee left, he came upon Matilda sitting with her head resting on the kitchen table.

"Whatever is the matter?" he asked. "Is Matilda not feeling well?"

"I have pain in my stomach," she replied.

Samuel laid his hand on her forehead. It was burning.

"Come and lie down," he said, helping her to her feet. "How long has it been going on?"

"Since this morning."

"Shall I send for the doctor?" he wondered.

"No, no. It will pass."

But it didn't pass. Samuel sat beside her all night, soothing her forehead with cold, wet towels. She was worse on Sunday, now and then losing consciousness. He sat beside her all day, visibly worried. She had never been sick in all the years they had been married. The only thing that had put her in bed was giving birth.

"If Matilda is not better by tomorrow morning, I'm going to send to town for Dr. Hagström," he told her.

He sat up beside her that night also. At daybreak on Monday morning, Emma went down to the telephone station in the village and placed a call to Dr. Hagström.

But when he arrived an hour later, it was already too late. Matilda had died while clutching Samuel's hand. The autopsy revealed a burst appendix.

Samuel was inconsolable.

"Why, God, have you let it end like this? What did we do wrong?" he cried over and over silently.

He was to ask the same questions hundreds of times in the twenty-nine years he had left to him, but he never received an answer...

...Samuel picked up Walter's letter and continued reading it half-heartedly. He appreciated his offer to go and live with him in America, but he knew he would never do it. For one thing, he couldn't leave Emma, nor would she go with him. Both she and Fritz had many times remarked that they had no desire to emigrate.

But most of all, he couldn't imagine abandoning the world that he and Matilda had shared. He felt her presence in the rooms and surroundings where they had lived together for thirty years. Every

Sunday, he walked several miles to church in the next village. It wasn't because of the service or the fact that they had worshipped there together their entire married life. Nor was it because of the proximity of her grave just outside the wooden building. It wasn't in these places that he felt her spirit. It was when he walked home on the path through the forest that they had always taken. Because it was too narrow to walk side by side, Samuel always went first "to scare away the vipers" that sometimes sunned on the rocks.

The path climbed upward through the trees to a ridge, on top of which the landscape suddenly opened up to the east. One could see so far that the horizon became just a dark line against the sky fifty miles away. The first time they saw the view they were over-whelmed. Simultaneously, they sank down side by side onto a large flat stone and gazed out in awe over the endless forest below them. Neither of them spoke, for there were no words for what they both felt. They simply sat like Siamese twins, joined where their shoulders touched, and let their feelings flow freely between them.

Finally, Samuel laid his hand over Matilda's where it rested on her lap, and they stood up.

"Now I know why I never find God inside the church," he said. "He's not there. He's out here in nature."

The experience had joined them in a silent bond that was to last the rest of their lives. Every Sunday, on their way home, they rested on the stone without speaking, as if to renew that bond.

Even after her death, Samuel continued to visit the ridge to marvel at the view, sitting on the stone alone, yet not alone. Matilda's spirit was so strong that he could almost feel the pressure of her shoulder and the warmth of her hand under his. At first, Emma tried to convince him to go with her to Fritz's church in another village, but he excused himself by saying that he felt more at home in his own parish church. His real reason was too private, too unmanly.

When Emma and Fritz married a few years later, Walter repeated his offer. This time, Samuel was forced to consider it. Emma was moving to Fritz's family farm, that he had taken over when his parents retired. In keeping with farming tradition, they had moved into the little cottage on the edge of the land which existed solely for that purpose. Consequently, there was no place for Samuel to live.

Just when he was about to write and accept Walter's offer, Beda, an old family friend, came to his rescue by offering to rent out her upstairs to him. This was no love affair. She was a widow and, like Samuel, couldn't imagine sharing her life with anyone else after her Jakob. But she liked the security of knowing that she was not alone in the house, especially at night. And because she had spent her younger years in America and had become somewhat fashion-conscious, she often came to Samuel with a piece of material she had come across and asked that he sew something according to her own design. In return, she saw to it that he had at least one warm meal a day as well as taking care of his washing and ironing.

When Fritz's parents died, it was natural that Samuel moved into the little cottage on their land. Once again, Emma cooked for her father and took care of his household needs. She tried to convince him to go to church with them, but he argued that he preferred to continue attending his old parish church where he felt at home, even though he now had farther to walk. He couldn't bring himself to speak of his meetings with Matilda.

By the time Fritz and Emma eventually bought a larger farm even farther from his parish church, Samuel was in his early eighties. Not only was there no cottage for him there, which meant that he would have to live in the main house with them, but it was too far for him to walk to the ridge. For twenty-nine years he had communed with his Matilda on their ridge every Sunday, except when the deep snow made it impossible, and he couldn't bring himself to stop. It was his lifeline. Reluctantly, he chose to move to the old people's home in his native village. Emma found his decision strange but knew her father well enough to understand that it was useless to argue with him.

The first Sunday after he had moved into the old people's home he set out as usual for the ridge after church. He hadn't reached the beginning of the path on the far side of the village before a nurse from the home, caught up with him. She grabbed him by the arm, jerking him to halt.

"Just where does Herr Nordström think he is going?" she demanded.

"I'm going to visit my wife," he replied innocently.

"Herr Nordström is not allowed to go home," she told him, ignoring his answer.

"I'm not going home, I'm going to visit my wife," he repeated.

"No one is allowed to go out walking without being accompanied by one of our nurses."

He jerked free of her grasp.

"Leave me alone! I do not need an escort when I visit my wife!" he declared.

Just then one of the men who worked at the home caught up with them and, in spite of his angry struggles to free himself from their grasps, they marched Samuel back to his room.

The next day he was diagnosed as being out of contact with reality and potentially dangerous. He was sent to a nearby mental hospital. A few days later he was discharged and returned to the old people's home.

The following Sunday he once again set off for the ridge. This time he was brought back by two strong men. When he protested that he was only going to meet his wife, he was told that she had been dead for thirty years.

"I know that," he wept in frustration, but no one appeared to hear him.

From then on, he was kept under close scrutiny. But when he failed to show up for dinner one day, a search party was sent out to find him. They returned empty-handed. He wasn't found until several days later when one of the maids went up into the attic to hang up the washing out of the rain. The first thing she saw when she reached the top of the stairs was his feet swaying gently above the floor as the wind passed through the attic window.

ALULF

The summer sun had already disappeared behind the slum's grimy tenement buildings, but the stifling heat remained like a curse over the city. A typical New York July. The half-melted asphalt oozed through the worn-out soles of Alulf's shoes. It wouldn't have burned more if he had been barefoot. He paused outside the door of the shabby bachelors hotel that had been his home for so many years, pushed his hat back off his forehead, and wiped the streams of sweat from his face with his coat sleeve.

Out of habit, he turned and looked behind him before lifting the sandwich board, which he had carried all day, from his shoulders. Then, with a sigh, he pulled open the door and went inside. After leaning the board in a corner of the hallway, he made his way slowly up the stairs to the fourth floor and his room. His legs were tired, and he felt much older than his sixty years. He had long ago tired of that sandwich board that was his livelihood.

Life had been better before the Depression, when he was working in the garment factory. In those days, he still had a few dollars left over for himself after he had sent money home to his family in Sweden. But since having lost his job a few years back, life was hard. Carrying a sandwich board didn't pay much. But luckily, as the hotel's handyman, he didn't have to pay rent and even got his dinner for free. So life wasn't completely unbearable.

He kicked off his shoes and stretched out on the iron bedstead's lumpy mattress, causing the naked springs to squeak like small mice. Outside the sooty half-open window, the red hotel sign was already lit and the sound of a passing freight train forced its way in over the windowsill. Alulf's eyes wandered around the little room, pausing over each of the few pieces of furniture: a wooden orange crate that served as a bedside table, a washstand holding an enameled washbasin and pitcher of water with a shaving mirror hanging on the wall above it, a bureau with three drawers, and a table with two spindle-backed chairs. The linoleum was threadbare, and the water-stained wallpaper had loosened in a number of places. Actually, it was unnecessary to have two chairs, since Alulf didn't know anyone well enough to invite them up. But the back of the extra one made an excellent hanger for his Sunday suit. He liked to look at it hanging there; it reminded him of a better life than that of every day. He closed his eyes with a sigh. Saturday evening, that little bridge between two realities, was always hard. And likewise Sunday evening, when the bridge went in the other direction.

His thoughts wandered back to the 1890s, the Sweden of his child-hood, when the whole family—his parents, his twin brother, Ulf, and his six younger sisters—slept together in a kitchen that wasn't much larger than his present room. He wondered how life had gone for them, if they had put to good use the money he had sent home every Christmas and Midsummer for almost forty years. Never had he gotten even the smallest thank you. At the same time, he was convinced that they had received his letters with the enclosed money; he had always written his return address on the back of the envelope, and none had ever been returned to him. Deep inside, he knew that his father lay behind the silence. He could still feel the wrath marching up his spine when he remembered that day...

The twins, Alf, as he was then called, [which means "elf" in Swedish] and Ulf (which means "wolf") were the oldest of the family's eight children. As fraternal twins, they were two distinct individuals. Ulf grew up to be big-boned and strong, but Alf didn't grow along with him. Instead, he remained small and rather frail. They were, in fact, like an elf and a wolf, a fact that their father had constantly assailed them with since early childhood. It didn't matter what Alf did, it was never good enough in his father's eyes. He only saw Ulf; Ulf who was biggest and strongest and best at everything, just as he himself was. Alf idolized Ulf for his strength but hated him as a brother—a brother who enjoyed belittling him cruelly whenever he had the chance. And, although he knew he would never succeed, he never gave up trying to win their father's attention away from his brother. Until that March day just after they had turned twenty.

On their way home from town that day, they had decided to take a shortcut across the little lake bordering the farm. They checked the ice by the dock. Since it still seemed to be thick under the previous day's snowfall, they set out walking straight across. After a couple hundred yards, Alf began to get nervous, both afraid to say something and afraid not to. Finally he took courage.

"Wait, Ulf," he said cautiously. "I think we should go a little more to the right in order to avoid the spring in the middle of the lake. The ice can be thin right there."

"Don't worry. I know what I'm doing, Baby Brother," Ulf answered, cocky as usual.

Alf knotted his fists in his jacket pockets. He detested that demeaning nickname everyone in the family used whenever he asserted himself. In protest, he fell a good bit behind Ulf.

Halfway across the lake, the sound of a dull crack echoed through the silence, and Ulf disappeared from sight. The first time he came to the surface, he screamed. The second time, he splashed hysterically, gasping for breath. Alf ran toward him, while yelling for help at the top of his lungs. Just as he had thought, there was a large hole in the ice where the somewhat warmer spring water flowed straight up through the lake. The ice around the edge of it was thick, as if having been cut by an ice fisherman.

Alf got down on all fours and crawled toward his brother. But when he was finally able to grasp Ulf's wildly waving hands, he realized he was powerless to pull Ulf up in his water-drenched clothes. Worse, he realized that Ulf would drag him down into the hole if he didn't let go of him. Neither of them could swim.

Paralyzed with fear, they looked at each other in the midst of their tug-of-war. What happened next remained forever between the two of them. When help finally came, it was too late. Ulf was gone, his fully clothed body having vanished under the ice.

Their father was in a frenzy.

"You drowned him!" he screamed when he finally caught up with

Alf in the woodshed. He pulled off his leather belt, forced Alf into a corner, and beat him with all his strength.

"You drowned him on purpose! You've always hated him! You've always been jealous of him because he was bigger and stronger—more clever—a better person than you'll ever be! I'll never forgive you! Never! You're nothing but a worthless good-for-nothing! I wish you had drowned instead!"

He continued to beat Alf wildly, unable to burn up his anger. He would gladly have beaten him to death, but Alf's thick homespun clothes protected him from the knife-like lashes, which only further inflamed his father's fury. He continued swinging his belt, striking blows wherever he could, until he was exhausted. Shaking and out of breath at last, he sank down onto the chopping block.

"Get out of here and don't ever come back!" he growled. "I never want to see your evil face again! If I do, I'll kill you!"

When his father closed his eyes to wipe the sweat from his face with his mitten, Alf ran past him and out the door. Without looking back, he kept on running along the path that led toward the road.

When Ulf's body came to the surface in the spring, Alf was already in America.

The first years in America were hard. New York had many immigrants who never got further than the city's various ethnic districts, where every language except for English was spoken. As a farm boy, Alf felt alone in the city, even though everyone in the neighborhood spoke Swedish. He longed for home. Most of all, he longed for the gentle encouragement his mother had always offered him. It had given him a tiny spark of faith in himself, in spite of his father's efforts to undermine any self-confidence he might have had.

But now, away from them both, the words that rang loudest in his head were the demeaning words his father had constantly shouted at him, words that had always been much louder than his mother's. Nor could he imagine what she would have found to say to him after that day on the ice. More and more he had understood that his father was right; he was a worthless good-for-nothing. He would never strike it rich and be able to return home with pockets full of dollars. Ulf could have done it, but not he. No, he would be glad if he didn't starve to death in the Promised Land.

At night Ulf appeared in his dreams, glaring at him accusingly and mouthing the word "murderer" over and over. And even though he hadn't actually forced Ulf under the water, he knew in his heart that he was guilty of murder. But while it was true that they had had their conflicts, at the same time, they were twins. The only thing that could have drawn them closer to each other would have been if they had been identical twins. As a means of honoring his brother and at the same time attempting to inherit a bit of his strength, he decided to put their names, and consequently their characters, together and call himself Alulf.

After a few lean years, Alulf finally got a steady job as a janitor in a large garment factory and, by living frugally, he was able to save a few dollars, which he sent home with his first letter. He was determined to make his father proud of him.

Beloved parents and sisters,

I am just sending these lines to let it be known that I am in good health and hope everyone at home is the same. I like it here in New York and have gotten a job in a factory that produces machine-made clothes. I'm enclosing a little money for Christmas, which can surely be of use, and will send more at Midsummer. I promise to continue to send money twice a year in the future to try to make up for the loss of the only two sons in the family.

I deeply regret what happened to Ulf. I did my best, but I couldn't pull him up. He was too heavy in his wet clothes. What is done cannot be undone. Can Father forgive me? Can God forgive me? Please, Father, I beg for thy forgiveness.

Your son, A. Erlingsson

On the back of the envelope he wrote simply, A. Erlingsson so as to avoid revealing that he had changed his name, and the address to the tenement house where he rented a room from a Swedish family. He waited for weeks, then months, for an answer, but no sign of life came from Sweden.

At Midsummer, he once again sent money and wrote that he was in good health and that everything was fine with him. And once again he begged his father fervently to forgive him. No answer came back.

The next Christmas he sent a little more money than before, to show that he had become even more successful. It wasn't actually the case, but he was desperate to win his father's forgiveness and acceptance. He had already understood that it wasn't possible to win him with words, but money should speak for itself. There was never any money at home, and he was prepared to sacrifice himself for their sake. If he could just send enough money, his father would be forced to acknowledge his capability and see that he wasn't the good-for-nothing he had accused him of being. Or so he thought. But no response came from Sweden.

When his Midsummer letter failed to soften his father, he began to scrimp and save in order to send even more money home the next time. Winning his father's forgiveness and praise had become an obsession.

The following Christmas he wrote that he had been promoted to a job with more responsibility and thus was able to send home a greater sum of money, thinking his father would be proud of him. In truth, he had simply scrimped and saved all autumn in order to be able to increase the size of the money order. But to no avail.

Eventually, he was able to move to a residential bachelors hotel in another part of the city. But although he was glad to be on his own at last, he missed the connection with the old country that he had felt in the Swedish neighborhood. Most of all, he missed his native language, for he felt like a stranger was using his mouth when he tried to speak English. Nevertheless, at first he did his best to learn from the people around him, but after being laughed at a number of times for his efforts, he gave up. He was by nature shy and withdrawn and soon became even more so. Nor had he any friends.

Each day after work, he came back to his bachelor's room and lay on his bed daydreaming about the nice Swedish girl he would one day meet. In his loneliness, she began to take form. He named her Rose-Marie. Some days she seemed so near that he could almost see her. Before long they were holding mental conversations in Swedish. He told her about his father and mother and Ulf, and she reciprocated with tales of her own family. Soon they were planning their future—where they would live, how many children they would have, what they would name them. They had no secrets from each other. He no longer felt lonely.

At first, he left her in his room when he went out. Thus he lived in two worlds; one outside his room when he went to work and the other inside his head when he was in his room. Both were equally real. Then gradually he began to take her with him when he went out, and his worlds slowly, lost their individual contours and eventually merged into one. And because she had been brought up in the old country and knew her place, Rose-Marie always kept herself in the background when around other people.

One day on his way home from the garment factory, he paused to look at some pictures of people and street scenes displayed in the window of a photographer's studio. Down in one corner of the window were a couple of box cameras for sale. The thought that a person could create such pictures with one of those little boxes fascinated him.

Every day for the next few weeks he studied the photos on his way home. Finally, one day he plucked up his courage and went inside.

"The little box," he began in his broken English. He pointed towards the window. "How much cost it?"

"Prata du svenska?" the man asked.

"*Ja!*" Alulf exclaimed excitedly.

It was the first time he had heard his own language spoken since he'd moved away from the Swedish quarter. He held out his hand.

"Alulf Nykvist from Bjurtjärn Parish."

"Isaksson. Hugo Isaksson. Kalv Parish," the man reciprocated, shaking his hand.

They chatted in Swedish, drawn to each other by the soft, sing-songy melody of their native language. It was the beginning of a friendship that would last many years, albeit governed by the formal reserve they had both brought with them from the old country.

"So Nykvist is interested in the box cameras?" Isaksson said finally.

Alulf nodded.

"They cost two dollars and thirty-seven cents. And then one needs film, of course, which costs a dime."

"Oh," Alulf replied. He had no idea how a camera functioned. He just knew that he wanted to capture people and places on paper.

Isaksson lifted one of the cameras out of the display window and set it on the counter in front of Alulf.

"Does Nykvist know how a camera functions?" he asked him.

Alulf shook his head.

"One holds it like this and looks through this little window," he instructed. "When the picture is centered, one must hold very still and gently push this button."

He went on to explain how to load the film, wind it, and take it out when it was finished.

Alulf stood spellbound, not uttering a word. When the man had finished his demonstration, he looked at him questioningly.

"I buy it," he said.

He dug in his pocket and pulled out a handful of loose change which he lay on the counter. Slowly he slid all the nickels into one group, all the dimes into another, and left the pennies in-between them. There were no quarters. When he had counted it all, it only came to a dollar ninety-eight. He shrugged and scooped the coins into his hand again and was about to drop them back into his pocket.

"Wait," Isaksson said, putting out his hand to stop him. "How long would it take to save the other forty-nine cents?"

Alulf shrugged again. He had already taken from the money he had put aside to send home come Midsummer.

"I'll tell you what," he continued. "I've seen Nykvist standing outside my window every day for the past month, so I know this is important to him. I will set the camera aside until Nykvist can get together forty cents more and then he can have it with the film included."

"Oh, many thanks, sir!" Alulf said happily. He held out his hand and they shook on the deal.

When Alulf awoke on Sunday morning, the July sun was already beating down on the city. The previous day he had made the final payment on the camera and now it stood on the table across from his bed, its lens aimed at him expectantly. He picked it up carefully, measuring its weight in his hand. Isaksson had helped him load the film, so it was ready to go. Quickly, he put on his Sunday suit, slid his fingers under the strap on the top of the box, and went downstairs to the street. He had long ago decided that he would take his first pictures at Coney Island.

The trolley was filled with families bearing picnic hampers and umbrellas, seeking to escape the heat of the city, and the beach was already crowded when they arrived. Alulf wandered aimlessly among the sunbathers and children, camera poised against his stomach, trying to decide what to photograph first. Then he saw it—an organ grinder with a monkey on a leash collecting coins in a tin cup. He looked down into the view-finder, but just as he placed his finger on the shutter button, a young woman, stepped between him and the organ grinder.

"Oh, sorry," she laughed, stepping back quickly when she realized her mistake.

But too late. His finger had already pressed the shutter to capture the monkey with its cup.

"It does nothing," he replied shrugging his shoulders.

The girl continued on her way, and Alulf took a picture of the organ grinder and the monkey, this time making sure no one was about to walk between them. He took a couple more pictures, then spent the rest of the day sitting on the beach watching people and enjoying the cooling sea breeze.

The following Saturday Alulf stopped by the photography studio to see if his pictures were ready.

"Oh, yes, they were finished a couple of days ago. I develop them myself right here," Isaksson told him, ducking into the room behind the curtain and returning with an envelope. "So if Nykvist ever wants extra copies or enlargements made, just let me know."

Alulf unfastened the little clip holding the envelope closed and slid the photos out onto the counter. There was the girl from Coney Island smiling up at him from the top of the pile!

"Oh!" he gasped.

"I say, she's quite a beauty," Isaksson commented. "I take it she's Nykvist's girlfriend," he added.

Alulf nodded, unable to take his eyes off the photo.

"What is her name, if I may ask?" he continued.

"Rose-Marie," Alulf heard himself say.

"That certainly suits her! Lucky man!"

"Thanks," Alulf replied, not daring to look up in his confusion. "How much do they cost?" he continued quickly.

Isaksson quoted the price, adding that Alulf also needed a new roll of film.

Alulf laid the money on the counter, collected his photos and film, and said a hasty good-bye. Once out on the sidewalk, he realized that he hadn't even looked at the rest of his pictures.

When he got back to his room, he emptied the envelope onto the table and stared at the girl.

"Rose-Marie," he murmured. "Rose-Marie."

He pulled out one of the thumbtacks holding up the peeling wallpaper and pinned the photo on the wall beside his bed, then lay back, hands behind his head, and gazed at it longingly.

Every Sunday for the rest of the summer, he returned to Coney Island and combed the beach for Rose-Marie. But he never found her. Come autumn she continued to fill his Sundays, even though he no longer went to the beach. He began exploring various parts of the city, often with her by his side. He always walked with his head slightly turned, so that Rose-Marie was just out of range of his peripheral vision. Sometimes he photographed a café where they had sat and drunk coffee or somewhere they went on an outing or a house that they would like to buy.

One Sunday, he saw a young woman dressed in a housemaid's uniform walking a little dog in Central Park. Rose-Marie! As she came nearer, he lifted his camera and clicked the shutter. When he looked up, he realized his mistake. Although she had blond hair and blue eyes and was pretty, she was not Rose-Marie. Hugo Isaksson, however, did not notice the difference when he printed the picture, for he had not spent hours studying her face.

"So how is Rose-Marie?" he asked, with a nod towards the envelope of new photos as he handed it to Alulf.

"Oh, she's fine," Alulf replied, emptying the contents of the envelope out onto the counter as usual. When he came to the picture of the woman, he paused. She actually did look a lot like Rose-Marie. He could feel Isaksson's silent questions.

"She's Swedish," Alulf told him, "and works as a housemaid for some rich people—cleans, irons, walks their dog. His name is Fritz." His voice began to tremble when he realized that he had no control over the words coming from his mouth.

Once again, he said a hasty good-bye and left the shop.

Back in his room, he pinned the two photos side by side on the wall and gazed at them, comparing what features he could discern in the tiny snapshots. Although they were two different women, for him they soon became simply two different aspects of Rose-Marie.

As Christmas neared, he asked Isaksson if he could make a

slightly larger copy of the Coney Island photo of Rose-Marie, to send home to Sweden.

"Keep this one," Isaksson told him when Alulf came to pick it up, "and give the smaller one to Nykvist's family. It's cheaper to send and besides, she is more important to him than to them."

He took Isaksson's advice. The larger photo was much nicer to look at when he laid in bed.

Along with the little picture and the Christmas money order to his family, he wrote:

> *Beloved Parents,*
>
> *As you see, I am sending a little more money than usual. I have gotten another promotion. And I have met a wonderful girl. She works as a housemaid for some rich people here. Her name is Rose-Marie and she comes from Bosebo Parish in Småland. I hope that soon I will have enough money so that we can get married.*
>
> *Father, I beg for your forgiveness for that which happened to Ulf. Please write soon.*
>
> *Your son, A. Erlingsson*

In reality, there wasn't much hope that he would ever rise above the position of janitor at the garment factory. They hardly knew he existed. But surely his father would be impressed.

Once again he waited for an answer. In vain.

Undaunted, he continued to send money home twice a year, often accompanied by a photo of some place he had gone with Rose-Marie.

One Sunday in June he awoke earlier than usual, full of excitement. As usual, his gaze fell on his good suit hanging over the back of the chair expectantly, having been thoroughly brushed the previous evening. Hanging over the back of the other chair was his only white shirt, with his tie draped over it. He got up and folded back the mattress to where his suit pants lay on newspapers to protect them from the naked bed springs while being pressed under his nightly weight. He dressed quickly, grabbed his camera on his way out of the room, and let the door slam behind him. At the bottom of the stairs, he pulled his Sunday hat down low over his forehead, hunched his shoulders, and stepped out onto the sidewalk. But as soon as he had rounded the corner at the end of the block, he straightened up, pushed his hat back, and walked as if he owned the world. Rose-Marie walked by his side. They had recently gotten married and were going to look for a flat in a better neighborhood.

A few weeks earlier he had photographed a newly married couple coming out of a church holding hands, with a crowd of people visible behind them. When Isaksson had printed it, he confronted Alulf half-jokingly.

"Has Nykvist lent his camera to someone else?"

"What does Isaksson mean?" Alulf asked innocently.

"That looks like Nykvist and his Rose-Marie coming out of church as man and wife," he said, indicating the tiny figures in the photo. "The photographer should have stood a little closer."

"I know. It's a shame. We got married a couple of weeks ago. Just a small wedding." He examined the photo more closely. "There are Rose-Marie's relatives behind us. My father thought it was a pity that they couldn't be here, but they can't afford such a journey. But he sent his blessing."

Alulf sighed as he remembered the conversation. Perhaps his father had given him his blessing, and the letter had just gotten lost in the mail. Surely he was pleased that his eldest son had found a nice Swedish girl.

He spent most of the day walking around in Brooklyn with Rose-Marie, searching for a house in a quiet neighborhood. At last they found what they were looking for: a well-kept brownstone for rent with a flower garden in the little front yard and shady trees lining the street.

"What does Rose-Marie think?" he asked.

"It's lovely," she answered. "It will feel like being back home when

I can dig in the earth and plant flowers once again."

He raised his camera and snapped a picture.

"Let's see what shops there are in the next block," he suggested.

They crossed the street, and as they ambled along the sidewalk looking in the various shop windows, he could feel her hand resting in the crook of his elbow. It felt good to have her by his side.

They walked for several more blocks, past a school, several churches, and a park with a little duck pond in the middle.

"It's a nice place to raise children," Rose-Marie remarked.

"Yes, and it seems to be a mixed area instead of being solely Italian or Irish or Greek," he observed.

"I wonder if there are any Swedes or Norwegians here," Rose-Marie said.

"It doesn't matter," he told her. "We have each other to talk to, and we will speak Swedish with our children."

The following Saturday, dressed properly in his Sunday suit, he returned to Brooklyn and rented a mailbox in the post office. In his next letter home, he informed his father that he and Rose-Marie had moved to a nicer neighborhood, giving the post office box number as his mailing address. Included with the letter and money order was a copy of the wedding photo, along with one of the brownstone.

"We live on the ground floor," he informed both Isaksson and his parents. "There is a little yard behind the building where we can grow potatoes."

"It looks nice," Isaksson commented enthusiastically when he saw the picture.

"Yes, it's a quiet neighborhood," Alulf told him. "And there are a couple of grocery stores, a butcher shop, a post office, and a church on the same street. And even a park. Rose-Marie loves it."

"Nykvist seems to be doing well for himself," Isaksson said. "Not everyone from the old country is so successful."

"My boss seems pleased with my work, and already I've had a couple of promotions," Alulf told him. In English he added, "I try to keep my nose clean and work hard." He wasn't quite sure what keeping his nose clean had to do with anything, but it made him feel important to be able to use such clichés in his limited English.

Every Sunday, Alulf performed the same ritual. He put on his good suit, which he periodically replaced with a newer one from the Salvation Army, took his camera, and went out with his hat pulled down low on his forehead. By the time he turned the corner at the end of the block, however, he had straightened up, pushed his hat back on his head, and held out his arm to Rose-Marie. Together, they walked around their new neighborhood, first stopping to check his post office box to see if he had gotten a letter from home. And each time he could see through the little window above the combination dial that the box was empty. Nevertheless, he opened it and stuck his hand in all the way to the back, just to make sure.

"It looks like Father's letter has gone astray," he commented to Rose-Marie. "I thought for sure it would be here today."

Then they continued their walk, pausing now and then so he could photograph street scenes and neighbors.

One Sunday, a year or so after they were married, they saw a baby carriage outside a drugstore. It was summer, and the baby was clad in only a diaper. He raised his camera and clicked the shutter.

"Wait till Isaksson sees what's on this roll of film," Alulf said when he left it to be developed the following Saturday.

Isaksson gave him a curious look.

"We have become a family," Alulf told him proudly. "Isaksson is the first person to see a photo of little Thomas. And, of course, I need a copy to send home. My parents were so excited when I told them we were expecting a baby! He's their first grandchild. I promised them a photo as soon as he was born."

And so the years passed. Those Saturdays that Alulf went to Isaksson's photo shop to leave his film or pick up the finished pictures were almost as special as his Sundays. He always dressed in his best suit and made sure his shoes were shined. As soon as he put on his suit coat, he felt different. Even though he never took Rose-Marie to the photo shop with him on those Saturdays, he walked with his head high, as though she were by his side. Even his step was lighter.

In time, there were more children. Dora. Fredrik. Alice. He photographed them all. There were moves to a larger flat and finally to a house on the outskirts of the city, with a new post office address. And because Alulf spent his Sundays in his new neighborhood, people there began to recognize him. They called him Camera Man, for although he smiled and waved, he never spoke. No one knew anything about him. They assumed he was a deaf-mute. The children, especially, liked him, for he often brought them small presents—a bag of candy or a ball or jump rope—to share. They willingly posed for him and sometimes he gave them copies of the pictures he had taken of them. He was accepted as part of the neighborhood, and they became his children. And his camera followed their progress as they grew up.

One Sunday, a motor car drove up the street and stopped across from the vacant lot where the children were playing. As soon as the driver disappeared into the drugstore on the corner, they ran over to have a look. Alulf raised his camera. Just as the oldest boy stroked the shiny black paint on the hood, he clicked the shutter.

"Wait till you see what I've bought!" he told Isaksson when he left the film to be developed. "Thomas was so excited when he saw it! Can you print an copy for me to send home to Sweden, please."

Isaksson was certainly impressed by the shiny new automobile.

"She's a real beauty!" he remarked when Alulf came to pick up his photos. "Nykvist has certainly been successful over the years. His father must be extremely proud."

"Oh, yes, he is!" Alulf assured him. "And he is so glad for the money I have sent home twice a year. Life is not so easy in the old country, as Isaksson knows. It would have been easier if the whole family had emigrated with me, but my father's parents refused to leave Sweden and he didn't feel he could go without them. But it feels good to be able to help them."

He scooped together his pictures, with the two copies of the automobile on top, and bid Isaksson good-bye.

Back in his room, he added one of the copies to the collection of photos tacked on the wall beside his bed. Lying back against the pillow, hands behind his head, he gazed at them: Rose-Marie on the beach, Rose-Marie walking the dog, their wedding, their first apartment, Thomas in the baby carriage, the house in the suburbs, the other children, numerous outings, and now the new car. He closed his eyes and could feel the steering wheel in his hands and hear the excited chatter of the children as he took them for a spin. Even Rose-Marie loved the new car and was so proud to sit by his side as they went for Sunday drives in the country.

He sat up, took out pen and paper, and began to write.

Beloved Parents,

Once again, it's time to write and send a little money. I have my health, thanks to God, and I hope that everyone at home is also well.

As Father and Mother can see from the enclosed photo, I have taken one more step upward in life and have gotten myself a brand new motor car. The children were so excited when I brought it home, especially Thomas, who is standing there with such a big smile on his face. In sunny weather, we often take a Sunday drive out into the countryside, as is the custom in this country.

Father, please forgive me for Ulf's death and write soon. Rose-Marie sends her warmest greetings to my entire family.

Your son,
A. Erlingsson

He took out the money order he had bought the previous day and folded it into the letter. In the thirty-five years that he had been sending money home, he had never really considered whether his parents were still living or not, nor what their economic circumstances might have become. In his relationship to them, time stood still. He was forever the son who had let his twin brother drown, the son begging his father to forgive him, the son begging his father to see him as someone worthwhile.

When America was hit by the Depression, like everyone else, Alulf's life changed overnight. The clothing factory came to a halt, and he lost his janitor's job. But because he had served the bachelors hotel as handyman for so many years, he was the only person there who understood the intricacies of its heating and electrical systems. Thus he was allowed to keep his room, even though he could not pay the rent. However, his dinner was no longer included. Instead, he was forced to join the long soup kitchen lines outside various charitable organizations. The little money he earned from occasional odd jobs he saved and sent home to his family in Sweden. Having empty pockets didn't bother him much; he had been nurtured on poverty.

Life got better when he eventually got the sandwich board job. Once more, he could pay his rent at the hotel and receive free dinners, which were much more nutritious than soup kitchen food. But the years of walking the sidewalks in every kind of weather, with the heavy wooden boards hanging over his shoulders, had taken their toll on his back and feet, as well as his general health. Nevertheless, he continued to live for Sundays, when he could put on his suit and step into another world, where sandwich boards didn't exist. He and Rose-Marie had long ago settled into middle-class life, with no more upward moves or new cars. He continued to follow the children with his camera. Gradually they grew up, graduated from school, and moved out into the world. He kept Isaksson informed as to their progress, although he took fewer pictures nowadays.

One summer day, he rushed into the camera shop full of excitement.

"Guess what!" he exclaimed. "I have become a grandfather!"

He set a roll of film on the counter with a proud bang.

"Be prepared to meet Thomas's son, Joseph."

"Congratulations!" Isaksson replied cheerfully, shaking his hand. "Has Nykvist written the good news to his parents?"

"Not yet. I'm waiting until I have a picture to send. Can Isaksson make two copies of the best one, please?"

"Of course. Come back in the middle of next week, Grandpa."

That Sunday Alulf had a surprise waiting for him when he stuck his hand into his post office box. Lying flat on the bottom of the box was a slip of paper informing him that he had a package, but that he would have to pick it up on a weekday when the window was open. Since no one but his father knew his post office address, it could only be from him. He was both curious and excited.

Monday afternoon he stopped parading a little earlier than usual and, leaving the sandwich board in a safe hiding place, took the subway out to the post office. He handed in the slip of paper at the window and was given a package the size of a shoe box. Despite the hot humid weather, he ran to catch the next train back into town. Once he had retrieved the boards and adjusted their weight on his shoulders, he hurried toward the hotel, anxious to discover what his father had sent him after all these years. But he wasn't used to being out with his boards during rush hour, and he found it difficult to maneuver his way through the crowds, especially with his hat pulled down almost over his eyes as usual. Finally, he had to push it back to wipe his brow. As he did so, a man across the street thought he looked familiar and began to follow him, unable to believe his eyes.

When Alulf got to the hotel, he paused, took his hat off, and wiped the sweat from his face with his sleeve. Then, as always before starting to free himself from the boards, he glanced behind him.

There stood Isaksson!

"I thought I recognized Nykvist..." he began, but Alulf had already crumpled to the ground between the boards. Hastily, Isaksson lifted them away and knelt beside him.

"It doesn't matter," he said, having instantly understood the past forty years. "I'm still Nykvist's friend. Let me help him up to his room."

He pulled the key from Alulf's pocket, took the package that he was still clutching, and started to lift him into a sitting position. But it was too late.

"It looks like a heart attack," the medic said when the ambulance arrived. "Do you know him?"

"Yes, I'm his cousin," Isaksson said instinctively. "I'm all he has."

He gave them his name and address, saying he would notify his relatives in Sweden and make other necessary arrangements.

When they had gone, he let himself into Alulf's room. He switched on the light and looked around. The wall beside the bed was covered with photos, all of them familiar to him. For a long time, he just sat and stared at it, letting all those years fall into a completely different pattern than the one he had been led to believe.

Finally, he decided he might as well open the package. Lifting the lid of the box, he saw that it was crammed with letters. On top of them was an envelope with the word "Alf" written on it. After a bit of hesitation, he tore it open and began reading.

Dear Alf,

I regret to tell you that Father passed away a few weeks ago at the great age of ninety-one. When going through his things, we came across this box of letters that you had written. Father never mentioned having ever heard from you. Since they were just addressed to him, we felt it was better to return them to you. As you see, he never opened any of them. Sadly, as far as he was concerned, you were as dead as Ulf. Why he bothered to save your letters instead of burning them, I will never know. We always wondered what happened to you, but we were forbidden to mention either you or Ulf. Nor do we know any more now, aside from the fact that you are still alive and living in New York. Our mother died some years ago, but I can tell you that she never forgot you in her prayers. I hope that you will write and let us know how your life has been all these years.

Your oldest sister,
Anna

By now the sky was dark, and the neon hotel sign outside the window had come on, casting an unreal light into the room. A train rumbled by outside the window and disappeared into the night. Isaksson found a piece of paper and pen in the drawer of the table and began to write:

Dear Anna,
My name is Hugo Isaksson. I was a friend of your brother's. I regret to tell you that he passed away today from a heart attack on his way home with the package of letters, which he had not yet opened. I am returning them to you because I suspect they can tell you more about his life in New York than I could, even though I have known him for many years. Also, I believe they contain the money that he always sent home to your family at Christmas and Midsummer.

I didn't know Alf socially, so to speak. We only met when he came into my camera shop to leave a film or pick up his prints. At those times he told me about his wife and children (whose photographs he included in his letters to your family), but I never had the opportunity to meet them. Unfortunately, I do not know where they are living. Alf's post office box was just a business address.

Alf was a fine man, and I always enjoyed his visits to my shop. I am going to miss him.

Sincerely,
Hugo Isaksson

The next day Isaksson mailed the shoe box of letters back to Sweden, without a return address. It was the only act of friendship left to him.

HILDA

Long rays from the setting sun slid under a layer of high, sandbar-ridged cirrocumulus clouds, reddening their undersides. The air was fragrant with newly warmed pine sap, mingled with the delicate hint of birch leaves about to unfold. On either side of me, fallow fields gave off their own special damp, almost swampy smell, and bits of new greenness were starting to sprout among the old raspberry canes and dried grass along their edges. I unzipped my jacket and let the gentle spring breeze open it while I walked along the path toward the neighboring farm.

Half a century earlier, this had been the road connecting my house to the farm where old Hilda now lived alone. In those days, roads followed the twists and turns of the earth's contours, but as cars began to replace horses and wagons, the roads were straightened to accommodate faster traffic. But rather than straighten the many curves in this one, a completely new stretch of road had been built on the far side of the field, leaving the old road to fade back into the landscape. Already it was reduced to two parallel footpaths separated by a ridge of coarse grass and wild flowers.

I tried to imagine a horse and wagon coming along behind me on its way up to Hilda's, loaded with sacks of grain or perhaps empty ten-gallon milk cans clanking together as it bumped over the uneven earth. I could almost hear it getting closer and closer, until I actually expected it to overtake me. But instead, a junky old American car rattled up the road on the far side of the field, jolting me back to the present.

It wasn't the first time I had been sucked into the past while out walking in the Swedish countryside, where I had been living for many years. Every one of the numerous old houses decorating the landscape has its own story to tell of the past and the people who have lived in it. Together they create an atmosphere that pulls one back in time, for they have never really become a part of the twentieth century. It isn't like in America, where "the old days" were a couple of hundred years ago, when the pioneers were settling the country. Here, the old way of life existed close to its original form from medieval times all the way to the post-war years. The Second World War, that is. Up until that time, the country was abundant with people who had no running water, no indoor toilets, no central heating, no telephones, no cars. But now, three decades later, those who were going to catch up with the modern world had caught up. Yet out in the countryside, there were many elderly people who were content to live in the old way to which they were accustomed.

As I neared Hilda's house, her dog barked from the back door porch.

"Hush, Lady." I yelled. "It's only me." But she was old and getting deaf, as well as more protective. She had tried to bite me once when I cycled past, so I had respect for her. Hilda claimed it was because she had a thing about bicyclists, but I didn't trust her even when I was walking.

The back door opened, and I heard Hilda's old lady voice order the dog into the house.

"Hello!" I called to her. "It's just me, out for a walk as usual."

"Oh, come in, come in! I was just going to have coffee. Surely you could drink a cup. I have freshly baked cinnamon buns. Still warm, they are. Lady, shut up and get in here!"

A door slammed somewhere inside the house, and Hilda stuck her head out the back door again. "Come on now. The beast is locked away," she laughed.

I am no great coffee drinker, but it was impossible to say no to her cinnamon buns. Kicking off my boots in the hall, I went into the kitchen. A fire was burning in the wood stove and the oven door was open, letting the warm air drift out into the room. On the counter, several hand-woven dishtowels hid baking sheets of buns from view, but nothing could hide their enticing aroma.

I sat down on the bench by the table and looked out the window. The sun was just pulling away from under the brilliant clouds and sinking below the black line of the horizon. Hilda placed cups and saucers on the oilcloth-covered table, added a shot of cold water to the coffee boiling in the pot to settle the grounds, and filled our cups. Replacing the pot on the edge of the wood stove, she returned with a plate of cinnamon buns in crinkly paper baking forms.

"*Var så god,*" she said, the inviting words one must wait for before taking that which has been set before one.

"Mmmmm!" I declared after the first bite. "These are wonder-ful!"

"Asch, they're too fresh!" she scoffed. "You can't dunk 'em in your coffee without having 'em fall apart."

She poured a bit of coffee into her saucer, placed a sugar cube between her front teeth, and sucked the rapidly cooling coffee through it. I had only seen men drink that way, but concluded that it was to compensate for not being able to dunk the bun.

Outside the window, the sky had finished its show and was start-ing to darken, but Hilda made no move to turn on the light. Neither of us said anything for a long time.

"It's so nice to sit quietly in the twilight like this," she said final-ly. "We call it *kura skymning* in Swedish. We always did it in the old days. We never lit the lamp until it was absolutely dark."

"Tell me about life in the old days," I said. "Were you born here, or did the farm belong to your husband's family?"

"No, it belonged to my mother's aunt and uncle. I came to live with them seventy-three years ago, when I was seven."

"Hmmm," I mused, trying to put those facts together into some sense. "I don't understand. Did something happen to your parents?"

"Oh, no, not at all. Things like that were rather common back then."

"How so?"

Hilda leaned back in her chair and sighed slightly. I could see by the faint light from the window that her eyes were closed.

"I was born in the next village," she began. "I had three older brothers and a sister who was two years older than I was, and then a baby sister. We lived right in the middle of the village, across from the school. My father worked for the railroad, and my mother sometimes did odd jobs for people. She helped at weddings and funerals, or with the big washings people did before Midsummer and Christmas. That sort of thing. One day when I was seven, my mother's old aunt and uncle came to visit unexpectedly. That day changed my whole life..."

The sun had not yet reached the attic window when Hilda woke up that morning. Usually, it was the warmth of it shining on the bed that woke her, but not today. Instead, it was the sound of voices coming from the kitchen below. She rolled onto her back, careful not to wake Dora, who was sleeping head to foot with her.

Outside the open window, the wind was blowing the little propellers off the maple tree, making them fly through the air like dragonflies. Her big brother Harry said there were seeds for new trees in them. She couldn't quite figure out how such tall trees could come from those teeny little seeds, but if Harry said it was so, then it was so. He was seventeen and knew things like that. Her other two brothers, Roland and Oskar, never told her interesting things. Mostly they teased her and acted stupid. As for her sister Dora, she liked to play with her when no one else was around. But as soon as Dora's school friends appeared, she was treated like a baby.

Hilda slipped out of bed, curious to find out who had come to visit so early in the day. Part way down the stairs, she was able to see an old woman in a long black dress sitting at the kitchen table drinking coffee with her parents. Coming down one more step, she saw a man on the far side of the table, also dressed in black. Something about them was familiar.

"I want to take Dora home with me," the woman was saying. "I'm getting old, and I need a maid to help with all that has to be done on the farm."

Immediately, Hilda recognized the voice of her mother's Aunt Amanda, who lived in the next village. She had never liked her. In fact, she was afraid of her. Amanda was very proper, and her mouth always seemed be pulled together as if she had eaten sour berries.

"Well, I don't know," her mother began slowly. "I need her myself."

"Take Hilda," she heard Harry say. "She's much nicer than Dora."

She snickered to herself, knowing he was joking. After all, she was only seven. Quietly, she retreated back upstairs to wake Dora.

"No! No! They can't take me!" Dora cried when Hilda told her what she had heard. "Usch! I don't want to live with those awful old people!"

"Not me, either!"

Without bothering to get dressed, they hurried down to the kitchen.

"Good morning, Mamma and Papa," they said nervously, trying to ignore Aunt Amanda and Uncle Gustaf.

"Good morning, girls," their mother answered. "Where are your manners? Or haven't you noticed that we have guests?"

They curtsied politely to the old people, then turned back to their mother, waiting for her to speak.

"Go upstairs and get dressed now," she told them. "It's not proper to go around half-dressed like that. Then go out and feed the animals and leave us adults to ourselves."

"But...," Dora began, but her father cut her off.

"Do as you're told!" He motioned them away with his hand.

Hilda was already considering the situation. Without her sister, she would have the whole bed to herself, and she wouldn't get punished for the things Dora did and blamed on her.

When they came back to the house after having fed the chickens and taken the cow out to the common grazing pasture, Amanda and Gustaf were getting ready to leave.

"Come along, Amanda," Gustaf prodded. "If we don't hurry, we'll miss the train."

They had walked the five miles from their farm to the train station and then would ride another five miles to attend a funeral in another parish.

"Have her things packed and ready by the time we get back from the service this afternoon," Amanda said in a tone close to an order.

"Yes, Auntie," their mother answered.

A train whistled in the distance. Gustaf steered his wife out the door and across the yard.

"Sit down and eat your breakfast," their mother told them. "Then we have to pack your things together, Hilda, so you can go with Aunt Amanda and Uncle Gustaf."

"Me?" Hilda cried. "I thought Dora was going."

"No, we decided that it would be better if you went. I need Dora to help me with the baby when I have to go and work. Besides, it's better if you start school there right from the beginning."

"School?" Ever since Dora had started school two years ago, she had looked forward impatiently to the day when she could go to school with her.

"Of course."

"In the summer?"

"No. But Amanda needs help all year round. And she is going to need more and more help the older she gets. Eat up now, so we can gather your things."

Hilda shoved her porridge bowl into the middle of the table.

"I'm not hungry," she said. "I don't want to go with them. I want to stay home!"

"Life is not a matter of doing what you want. If you're finished eating, let's get your things together."

Too proud to admit her hunger, Hilda left the table.

From her bride's chest where she kept the linen sheets, hand-woven years ago for her trousseau, her mother took out a big piece of brown paper she had been saving. Smoothing it out on the kitchen table, she began laying Hilda's clothes on it: her other dress, her two pinafores, a sweater, and an old jacket that no longer fit Dora. When Hilda saw her long, hand-knit wool stockings and her shoes added to the pile, she knew she was going for a long time. She only wore shoes and stockings in the winter when there was a lot of snow. Otherwise she went barefoot.

By the time Amanda and Gustaf returned that afternoon, Hilda was washed and her hair brushed and pulled into tight braids. Her bundle of clothes lay on the table, wrapped in the brown paper and tied securely with a couple of rounds of thin string. Only her mother and brothers were there to say good-bye. Dora had gone off to tell her friends of her narrow escape, and her father had gone to work.

"Be good and do what Aunt Amanda and Uncle Gustaf tell you," her mother told her. "We'll come to see you as soon as we have a chance."

She gave her a quick hug. Harry took a step toward her and stretched out his hand to pat her on the head, but she turned away and pulled her bundle from the table. Without looking at him, she stalked out the door and down the path after Amanda and Gustaf.

The first part of the way "home" was along the dirt road, which wound up and over the ridge between the two villages. Once they reached the top of the ridge, they cut off onto a footpath through the forest. Here they had to walk single file, with Gustaf leading the way. Amanda followed, carefully holding up her long skirt so as not to tramp on it as she stepped over the many rocks and roots. Last came Hilda, clutching her bundle against her stomach while trying not to stub her bare toes. Not only were her strides short compared to those of the adults, but her legs were also bowed as the result of having had rickets. Nor was she used to walking long distances.

Every once in a while, one of them, turned around to make sure she was coming. If she was too far behind, Amanda would stop and rest until she had almost caught up and then go on. Hilda never got a chance to stop and catch her breath for even a few seconds.

The bundle grew heavier and heavier. She tried carrying it by the string, but it cut through her fingers, even though she switched it back and forth from one hand to the other. And her legs ached so that she could hardly lift them. Finally, she sat down on a rock beside the path with the bundle on her knees. Amanda had disappeared from sight. The tears that she had held back all day suddenly overpowered her. If only one of them would come back and help her with the bundle, but neither of them appeared. Hilda rubbed her eyes with her clinched fists, smearing dirt across her face. Suddenly she was afraid. She had never been alone in the forest. Think if the wolves found her. She knew there were wolves, for she had heard a neighbor telling her father how they had killed one of his sheep.

Presently, she heard a rustling sound beside her. Turning, she saw the hem of Amanda's black skirt brushing the pine needles in the path. Slowly, she looked up. Amanda stood, hands on her hips, looking down at her. Her gray-streaked hair was pulled back to the knot at the nape of her neck so tightly that her face looked abnormally large and pasty.

"Get up," she said. "We haven't got all day."

Hilda turned around to pick up her bundle.

"Please, can you carry this for a while?" she asked, but Amanda didn't hear her. She was already on her way down the path again. It was evening by the time the three of them reached the farm.

Like all other farmhouses of its time and size, Amanda's and Gustaf's house was just a cottage, consisting of a kitchen and "best room" downstairs and an unfinished attic upstairs. The best room was just that—a room that was only used on special occasions and otherwise closed off from the rest of the house. Daily life took place in the kitchen. Everyone washed at the washstand just inside the door, and, at night, the wooden seats of the two sofas were lifted and the box-like, under-portions pulled out into beds. When tramps came past on their wanderings, they slept on the kitchen floor. Privacy was not an aspect of peasant life.

"Leave your things there," Amanda instructed, pointing to the box sofa by the kitchen table. Hilda hoisted her bundle up onto the seat and climbed up beside it. Amanda and Gustaf stood, one at each end of the room, with their backs to each other and removed their church clothes piece by piece, replacing each garment with a similar, but well-worn, one.

"Come on," Amanda told her when she had finished changing

her clothes. "This is no time to lie around. We have work to do."

Reluctantly, Hilda slid off the sofa and followed Amanda out to the barn. Without any introduction, she was handed a three-legged stool and a pail.

"This is how you milk a cow," Amanda said simply. Placing her calloused hand over Hilda's tiny one, she demonstrated how to draw the milk down into the teat and squeeze it out. "This will be your job every morning and evening. My hands are too crippled to do it any longer."

Hilda looked more closely at the hands covering her own. The fingers were warped and bent at a strange angle. She shivered. They looked just like witch's claws.

By the time the five cows had been milked, the dung shoveled out, and the milk cooled in the well of cold water in the floor, Hilda was so exhausted that she could hardly eat the oatmeal which comprised their evening meal. As soon as their bowls and spoons had been washed, Amanda drew the curtains across the windows to shut out as much of the summer light as possible. She and Gustaf pulled on their nightclothes over their heads and undressed underneath them. Then Gustaf tipped up the seat of the sofa by the window, set the peg in place to hold it up, and together they pulled out the box section.

"Where's my room?" Hilda asked timidly.

"Your room?" Amanda replied. "You sleep in the sofa bed by the table. You don't need to pull it out. For the time being, you can keep your clothes at the foot end, since your feet don't reach that far."

Hilda understood that no one was going to help her lift the heavy wooden seat. It took all her strength to raise it enough so she could step into the box underneath and push it the rest of the way up against the back of the sofa. But before she managed to fit the peg into the hole it fell back down, knocking her out of the bed and against the table. She cried out from pain and surprise.

"Hush, child," she heard Gustaf say. "Let a person get a little sleep."

This time Hilda didn't try to lift the seat high enough to fasten it. Instead, she raised it just enough so she could squeeze underneath and fall onto the straw mattress inside. Gently she let it close above her head and cried herself to sleep.

And thus began Hilda's life as maidservant. Amanda schooled her meticulously as to how to make a fire in the kitchen stove without having it smoke, how to grind and boil coffee, bake, polish the copper pans, clean the silverware with sand, knit, sew her own clothes, take care of animals—in short, everything that a farm woman needed to know. And as soon as Hilda had mastered a job, it was added to her list of everyday tasks. The first of these was to get up early every morning, make the fire, and have the coffee ready by the time the old people got out of bed.

When she complained, it was pointed out that when Amanda and Gustaf were children in the middle of the 1800s, most seven-year-olds had to go to work, usually for strangers. Often they had to live in the barn or a cold attic, get up at three a.m. and work until eight or nine in the evening. If they were lucky, they went to school every other day for a couple of months in the wintertime. Hilda had already heard the same thing from her grandmother, but it still didn't make her feel any better.

However, the times had changed in regard to school. One autumn day, a boy from the neighboring farm knocked on the door.

"My-name's-Arvid-and-my-mother-sent-me-to-say-that-we-can-walk-to-school-together-tomorrow-so-that-I-can-show-you-the-way," he said as fast as he could. As the last word left his mouth, he turned and ran down the hill toward home again.

Hilda's heart skipped a beat, not because of the boy, but because all summer she had feared that, with so many chores dealt out to her, she wouldn't have time to go to school.

It was a four-mile walk along windy wagon tracks and forest paths to get to school. At first, it seemed endlessly long, but after awhile, Hilda became accustomed to it. Then came the dark, cold, rainy days of November when her leather boots were soaking wet long before they reached the schoolhouse, as was her thin woolen coat. Nor was the classroom particularly warm. Her feet were always freezing in her wet boots, and to take them off was not allowed.

When winter came, they often had to wade through hip-deep snow, taking turns forging a path. By the time they got home in the afternoons, she was frozen clear through. But before she had a chance to get warm, it was time to do the milking. Sitting on the milk stool, sniffling against a warm, soft cow flank, she longed to go home to her family. There, she would simply have to cross the road to get to school, and she only had a few simple chores to do. Why did she have to live with these old people? They never laughed and had fun. They just smelled bad and snored all night. And ordered her around.

The years passed, and increasing responsibility fell onto Hilda's shoulders. Gustaf had a stroke that left him bedridden. Amanda's rheumatism became progressively more crippling. Although Sweden did not fight in the First World War, times were hard and food scarce. Their livelihood depended on what they could raise themselves, their only source of income coming from milk and the cheese and butter they made and sold locally.

Hilda's days were full to overflowing. Over the years, she had rarely seen her parents or brothers and sisters, for they lived in a different parish and thus they did not meet at church or social events. Gradually, they had taken on the guise of distant relatives, and her longing had ceased.

At the same time, daily life brought her into closer contact with Arvid and his family, until they replaced the one she had lost. She and Arvid were inseparable, even after they no longer walked to school together, so no one was surprised when, in their early twenties, they became engaged.

When they married, Amanda sold the farm to them and she and Gustaf moved into an old people's home. At last, Hilda was mistress of her own home and had a helpmate. The children came one after the other, five in a dozen years.

She set out to create for them, what she had missed—a real family. She had never been so happy.

Then one day, Arvid got sick. The local doctor was puzzled and sent him to the hospital for tests. There he was diagnosed with cancer and never returned home. Within a month, he was dead. Hilda was left a widow at thirty-nine, her oldest child fifteen, and the youngest three. And another world war on the horizon.

"How did you ever manage?" I asked in wonder. I knew all her children; they were a light-hearted bunch always ready to laugh. They certainly didn't give the impression of having had a deprived childhood. And Hilda herself was the most joyful of them all.

"When Arvid died, I realized that you can either count your blessings and be happy, or you can count your misfortunes and be miserable. Arvid and the kids were such a blessing in my life that they made my misfortunes insignificant. I already knew how to run this farm alone, but this time I had many small hands that helped me.

We were a family, and we were doing it for us—and for Arvid. It was as if he were always there watching over us and encouraging us when times got hard. The only other alternative was to put the kids in foster homes. But I had already lost my family once, and I had vowed never to let it happen again."

She got up automatically to put more wood on the fire. Before she could close the firebox door, it flared, sending a flickering light dancing out into the otherwise dark kitchen. She lit a candle and picked up the coffee pot.

"How about some more coffee and another bun?" she said with a laugh.

ELIN AND TEO

The path up to the top of the ridge felt steeper than usual in the June heat. Elin held up the skirt of her ankle-length cotton dress with one hand so as not to tramp on the hem, while gripping the handle of her empty basket with the other. She wished she had stayed home.

Usually, she traded her eggs and freshly churned butter for coffee and flour and perhaps a little sugar in the village store. But now, with wartime rationing, such things had disappeared from the shelves. All she came away with were the well-meant condolences over the death of her father from the villagers she had met. She felt like a hypocrite.

Her father had been a preacher in the fundamentalist chapel in the nearby mining village. As a young man, he had broken away from the state church, which he found too lax, and gathered his own following. That he had never been ordained into the ministry was immaterial. His hellfire and damnation sermons, delivered with the aid of his fiery black Walloon eyes, hypnotized his congregation of miners, farmhands, and common laborers and convinced them that their salvation lay in accepting his teachings.

Although Elin was also one of them, they set her a bit above themselves, for she was the chapel's organist, a job she had inherited after her mother's death a decade earlier.

The landowners and upper-class mine officials, on the other hand, attended the Swedish State Church in town. Not only was fundamentalism too low-class for their tastes, but in their eyes, Pastor Adamsson's self-righteousness showed a lack of respect toward his superiors. However, they themselves showed a certain respect for Elin, whose purity was equal to that of their own young women, by nodding when they passed her in the village.

At the top of the ridge, she paused to breathe in the fragrance of the Queen Anne's lace, relieved to escape the villagers' sympathy. It only intensified her guilt. Those who had over the years observed her and her father walking to and from the chapel every Sunday, or had noted their interaction during the service, looked upon them as possessing a model father-daughter relationship. No one suspected the truth.

As a so-called "afterthought," Elin was born long after her four older sisters. Her father ruled over her with an iron hand, thanks to her oldest sister Amalia. One night, a year after Amalia had left home to work as a housemaid, she had reappeared at the door with a bastard infant in her arms.

Horrified, their father hid her and the child in the attic. As soon as darkness fell the following night, he hurried her into the shed where he forced her to lie with the child on the floor of the farm wagon. In the event that they might meet someone, he tossed a couple of grain sacks over them. Then his whip snapped violently across the unsuspecting horse's rump, causing it to set off at a run with the wagon jerking behind it. When he returned the next afternoon, both he and the horse were exhausted.

His only comment was to forbid the rest of the family to ever mention Amalia again. At the same time, he commanded his wife to burn her belongings and to cut every trace of her from the photo album. He himself eradicated her name from the family Bible with a thick black line, placing a small cross and the year, 1920, after it.

To ensure that his shame remained hidden, he took a job in the mining village several hundred miles to the north, where the family was unknown. There, he gathered a flock of wayward miners in need of salvation. With the force of his voice and the power of his conviction, he inspired them to build a chapel and place him behind the pulpit and his wife behind the organ. His four daughters sang in the choir. Amalia had ceased to exist. Never again would he permit such sinfulness to touch his family. Consequently, Elin grew up under the hand of his crushing control. Above all else, she was taught to fear the wrath of God and to unquestioningly obey His mouthpiece, her father.

Now as she walked along the heather-lined path, unwelcome

thoughts floated to the surface. She began walking faster to escape them, but instead, they intensified. Her father was dead, a victim of the Spanish flu that had followed on the heels of the Great War. It had reaped a goodly number of lives in the village, including both the Methodist and Pentecostal pastors. When the epidemic appeared to have abated, Pastor Adamsson maintained that he was spared because only he preached the true word of God. Shortly after that announcement, he was stricken in the middle of the night and died two days later.

Yet it wasn't his sudden death that upset Elin, but rather the wave of relief that had washed over her in the instant she realized he was gone. Not only did she experience a deep shame over her relief, but she was frightened by the thought that both her father and God were watching her from afar and knew her innermost thoughts. She had grown up knowing that they were watching her day and night, but until now, she had never had anything to hide. Suddenly, she was shocked by the intense dislike that she felt toward her father.

"But I mustn't hate my father," she told herself.

"Why not?" replied an unfamiliar voice from within her.

"Because he's my father. One must love one's father and mother."

"But he has dominated you your whole life."

"It's a father's duty to protect his daughters," she reasoned.

"He hasn't protected you; he has stifled you. And since your mother died, he has been a tyrant. 'Elin, do this!' 'Elin, bring me that!' 'Don't wear your blue dress!' 'Pull your hair back tighter!' 'You are not to associate with so-and-so!' 'Cast your eyes down in front of men! It is provocative to look at them!' And remember how he drove Holger away when he came courting. There was never a finer Christian than Holger. He has been a wonderful husband to Greta, even though he would rather have married you."

"Stop!" she cried aloud. "I never wanted to get married anyway!"

Elin could still hear her mother's warning words: "Marriage is like being in prison. One has no freedom. And then there is that disgusting business at night! Burning in hell can't be worse than that! And then having to go through the horrible process of giving birth to babies that you don't even want! Stay away from men! They only want one thing!"

Sitting on the half-way-rock to rest in the heat, she pushed the ping-pong conversation from her mind, only to have the empty space filled with thoughts of enjoying life without her father. Sinful thoughts. How nice it was going to be not to have to tend to his needs. Selfish thoughts, full of guilt. She jumped to her feet and hurried toward home, but she could not out-distance the voices in her head.

As she neared the house, she could make out a child sitting on her front step. Coming closer, she recognized Little Sara, whose family worked on Ekbom's estate. Not only was Squire Ekbom Elin's landlord, but he was also the social welfare representative for the area. Little Sara often had to run unpleasant errands for him.

The child stood up and curtsied to Elin.

"Did the squire send you?" Elin asked her.

"A-a-a, yes," she answered nervously.

"And?" Elin said.

"He said to tell Elin that he is sending a man to fetch Elin's two cows tomorrow," she said hurriedly.

"What is it you are saying, child?" Elin declared.

"He said to tell Elin that he needs his pastureland himself," Sara repeated importantly.

"And I need my two cows for my livelihood," Elin muttered.

"Shall I tell him that?" Sara asked.

"Tell him I shall pay him a visit tomorrow," she said.

"Yes, ma'am," Sara promised.

Elin watched her skip down the path, barefoot and carefree.

"Watch out for snakes!" she couldn't help calling after her.

Her beloved cows! How could she live without them? They were her source of income: the milk, cream, butter, and cheese that she sold. Together with her eggs, it was all she had in the way of "cash." She must go to Squire Ekbom and plead, but she knew it would do no good. He had a reputation for being cruel and completely unsympathetic. And like all his renters sprinkled though his forestland, she was afraid of him. And with good reason.

By the next morning, her newly acknowledged dislike for her father had been replaced by a childlike longing for the security of his presence. As a *"hemmadotter,"* whose duty it had been to remain unmarried and care for her parents in their old age, her adult life had been centered around the running of the household. The workings of the world beyond her doorstep were as incomprehensible to her as that of a foreign government. And now, after a sleepless night, she forced herself to lift the latch of Ekbom's iron gate and enter that unknown world beyond the gate of the estate house. Alone. Although the sky was overcast, with a cool wind out of the north, Elin could feel small trickles of sweat running along her spine, sticking her cotton dress to her back.

A maid opened the servants' entrance with a slight nod of recognition. Elin followed her along a dark corridor to the back room that served as Squire Ekbom's office, keeping her eyes downcast out of nervousness rather than respect. After the maid's light knock on the door, she was ushered into the darkened room, and the door closed behind her. In front of her sat Squire Ekbom behind a massive oak desk. He continued writing in a ledger, ignoring her presence. Elin fidgeted, shifting her weight from one foot to the other while waiting for him to take notice of her.

It was well known that he enjoyed letting people stand before him and wait, increasing their anxiety and thus his power over them. But in spite of knowing that, she was unable to still her twisting hands under her apron.

At last, he snapped the ledger shut and looked up.

"Well, if it isn't God's Holy Servant!" he remarked with a sardonic grin. "And what does she want?"

"I-I-I..." she stammered.

"Hurry up! I have other things to do today!" he barked.

Elin took a deep breath.

"I've come to ask Squire Ekbom to permit me to keep my cows," she replied, squeezing out the words as fast as she could as she exhaled.

"She has no need of cows in the poorhouse," he told her matter-of-factly.

"The poorhouse?" she gasped.

"Yes, the poorhouse," he mocked. "Has Elin forgotten that employment on the estate and the cottage go together, and that when the man of the house can no longer work due to illness, old age, or death, the family no longer has the right to remain in the cottage? That's how it's been since the beginning of time, wherever one goes. With no exceptions. Not even for one of God's Chosen Few."

"But the poorhouse...," Elin began.

"Has Elin anywhere else to go? To her sisters in America? Or to Amalia perhaps?"

At the mention of her oldest sister's name, Elin understood that others than just God and her father were watching her. Without so much as a good-bye, she ran from the room and along the back hall to the kitchen door.

Once outside, she forced herself to slow down to a walk until she was out of sight of the estate house. How had he known about Amalia? In all the years since moving to the mining village she had not once let herself think about her sister for fear she would some-how give away her family's secret. If Squire Ekbom knew about her, how many other people knew? And what else did they know?

She felt as though she had been cut wide open and her innards exposed to public view. For the first time in her life she was completely alone, with no one to turn to for comfort or advice.

The following afternoon while Elin was hanging up her washing on the line between the two apple trees, she caught sight of an unfamiliar man coming along the path from the village. Her cows! He was coming to fetch her cows! As he neared the cottage, to her relief she saw that he was carrying a cardboard suitcase. Of course! He must be one of the tramps who went from cottage to cottage selling items from his suitcase: pins and needles, combs, small mirrors, buttons, shoelaces, soap, handkerchiefs, and such like.

Without a word, he set his suitcase down between them. Fumbling in his jacket pocket, he pulled out a folded paper and handed it to her, motioning her to open it.

"This is Teo Stensson," it read. "He returned from many years at sea only to find that his parents are dead and the family farm sold, so he has no place to live. Since Elin does not want to move from her cottage, I am sending him to live with her. He can do odd jobs in exchange for food and lodging. Locally, he is known as Döv-Teo because he is both deaf and dumb, although he can read and write. A. K. Ekbom."

She looked up from the letter to the tall, thin figure in front of her. His suit was shiny and frayed around the edges from years of wear, but it was clean and had all its buttons. Under his coat, his vest was buttoned up over a collarless white shirt. His clean-shaven face bore a friendly smile below a seaman's cap. But all that Elin saw was that he was a stranger and a man and thus dangerous. Instinctively, she backed away.

"Herr Stensson cannot lodge here!" she declared. "Give me that pencil."

He looked at her and shrugged his shoulders.

With tears of frustration pressing behind her eyes, she hurried into the cottage after her own pencil. But when she turned around to go out again, he was blocking the door.

"Go away!" she screamed, but he remained standing in the doorway.

With shaking hands, she smoothed Ekbom's letter facedown on the table.

"He cannot live here!" she scribbled. "There is no place for him to sleep. And what will people say!"

She handed it to him and shooed him in the direction of the estate house.

Two hours later, he was back with a new letter. He didn't bother to knock.

"He can sleep in the sofa-bed in the kitchen just as Elin does.

People will say that it's about time Elin had a man in her bed. There is no room in the poorhouse for either Elin or Teo. A.K. Ekbom."

Her father had always maintained that Squire Ekbom was possessed by the devil, but this went beyond anything she could imagine. She crumpled the letter and let it fall to the floor, then covered her face with her hands. And all the while Döv-Teo stood in the middle of the room staring at her.

By now it was too late to send him back with another letter. Grudgingly, she divided the porridge she had saved from breakfast and shoved his portion across the table to him. Bowing her head over her plate, she mumbled a prayer. Teo, too, bowed his head, but kept one eye on her so as to know when she was finished. They ate in silence, so unlike mealtimes with her father, who had bombarded her with his fanatical preachings as they ate. As much as she had hated having to listen to him, she found herself longing to have him across the table from her now rather than this deaf-mute stranger.

Once their meager meal was finished, Teo pushed his chair away from the table noisily, crossed his legs, and lit his pipe. Billows of sharp-smelling smoke rose to the ceiling and floated out across the unpainted boards in search of an escape route. For Elin, there was no escape route. She waved her arms at him wildly to indicate that he should go outside to smoke, but he was gazing out the window, lost in his own thoughts.

A helpless rage boiled up inside her, toward her father who had died and left her on her own, toward Squire Ekbom for having forced Teo on her, and toward Teo for having invaded her life. Quickly, she set the copper dishpan on the wood stove, so violently that the water splashed over the edge onto the hot stove with an angry hiss. A cloud of steam rose to the ceiling, mixing with the tobacco smoke, but because he had his back to her, Teo was oblivious to her angry outburst.

She washed the dishes mechanically—two cups, two bowls, two spoons—just as she had done when her father lived. It wasn't having a stranger in the house that upset her. Like all country people, her family had often taken in passing travelers for the night. One was obliged by law to do so in the days when inns were few and far between, and the tradition had lived on. Such travelers arrived late in the evening and slept on the floor, rolled up in their own blankets, thankful for a roof over their heads against the weather and a door closed against the wolves. And they continued on their way at the break of dawn, leaving a few welcomed copper coins in payment for the night's floor space. Elin was used to that sort of lack of privacy. But her father had always been there, creating an air of respect. But now she was faced with being alone with a man—and a stranger at that.

As soon as Teo stepped outside to relieve himself "around the corner," Elin draped her long nightgown over herself and quickly pulled off her clothes under its protecting tent. Everyone, religious or not, knew it was sinful to cast their eyes on a naked body, including one's own. Even husbands and wives never saw each other naked, regardless of how many offspring they had created under the bedclothes. Elin's entire family had always slept together in the cottage's single room, having imbibed discretion with their mother's milk. As the only male in the family, her father had slept in his long underwear winter and summer that, like most men, he only changed when he bathed a couple of times a year.

But Teo seemed indifferent to such sinfulness. Without so much as turning his back, he stripped off his clothes and laid them neatly on a chair. Long underwear was not a part of his garb. Elin lay in bed on the far side of the room transfixed, unable to prevent her eyes from following him as he moved around the room. His pale skin glistened in the summer twilight.

But it was the appendage which bounced gently between his legs that hypnotized her. Of course, she had known that males were different from females. As a young girl, she had seen a bull mount one of their cows and jab at it with what the local boys called his spear. But she had no idea what a human spear looked like.

In the same instant, she realized she was staring at a naked man! Horrified, she pulled the covers over her head and prayed for forgiveness. Unaware of the drama playing itself out across the room from him, Teo slid into bed and fell asleep as soon as his head touched the pillow.

Elin, on the other hand, lay awake until sunrise, weeping and chastising herself for her sinful behavior. What if her father were watching from up in heaven.

The next morning Elin was woken by the sound of splitting wood. It couldn't have been more than four o'clock, for the sun was just riding on the treetops to the northeast. Pulling back the curtain, she saw Teo lift the ax above his head and bring it down on a piece of birch standing upright on the chopping block. His shirt was draped limply over the end of the nearby sawhorse, giving the long rays of the rising sun the freedom to play across the sinewy ridges on his back, while rivulets of sweat glistened in the morning light. She could almost imagine how it would feel to run her hand over the smoothness of his skin.

"Dear Jesus," she whimpered, bowing her head, "deliver me from my sinfulness." But when she realized her eyes had remained open, still focused on the half-naked figure beyond the window, she was horrified. "Oh my God! I must be possessed by the devil!" she cried into the empty room.

She had to force herself to turn away from the window and light the stove. With fumbling hands, she dumped a spoonful of rye kernels, which served as ersatz coffee, into the roaster and set it on the stove. Once they were browned, she ground them into a coarse powder with a small stone, then boiled them.

Just as she set the ersatz coffee and a frying pan with potatoes and herring on the table, she caught sight of Teo buttoning his shirt while walking toward the cottage. With a brief nod, he sat down to his waiting breakfast. Elin remained standing by the stove, coffee cup in hand, staring at the floor. Her face burned at the memory of his naked body.

Teo ate quickly, mouthed his thanks with a smile and went back out to work. Pulling back the curtain, Elin watched him begin chopping again, waiting for him to remove his shirt. But a cloud had covered the sun, chilling the air. After a few minutes, she turned from the window and began the day's chores, fast resolved to ignore him as much as possible.

That evening, in spite of her best intentions, she once again found her eyes following Teo's movements as he undressed. The sight of his nakedness caused a tingling sensation in the pit of her stomach, yet she couldn't bring herself to look away. And thus the days and nights continued. One part of Elin wanted Teo out of her home and her life, while another part of her began to look forward to nighttime.

Teo, for his part, kept busy with the jobs that Elin's father had always taken care of outside: cutting trees, sawing and splitting wood for the coming winter, cutting hay for the two cows. Having grown up on a small farm, he knew, without being told, what needed to be done. Elin was thankful, realizing that she could never have gone on living there by herself. And because Teo apparently had never learned how to communicate, aside from a few practical signs, she was not bothered with having to converse with him. They lived in a silent harmony, neither knowing the other. Nor was she bothered by her attraction to him during the daytime when he was fully clothed. It was when he undressed for bed that the devil took over her soul.

Soon, she began dreaming about him, that she was sliding her hand over his back (the word caress was not part of her vocabulary). The next night her hand had moved to his chest and stomach. She could feel his skin under her fingertips. Then one night she dreamed that she held his spear cupped in her hand. It was soft and warm, nothing like the spear she had seen on the bull. She found herself wondering what to do with it, but before she reached any conclusion, she awoke with a start.

Looking across the room, she noticed that he, too, had woken up. She watched as he threw back the covers and stepped onto the floor. To her horror, his spear no longer dangled loosely between his legs. It stood straight up, swaying slightly as it curved upwards towards his belly. It was huge!

Elin's lower abdomen tightened automatically. Suddenly, she was frightened. Think if he jabbed at her like the bull on the cow. She was too vulnerable in bed in her nightgown. As soon as he went out to relieve himself around the corner of the cottage, she got up and hastily put on her clothes.

Her hands were shaking. She was beginning to think that he was in cahoots with the devil, that he had been sent to test the strength of her religious conviction. Or perhaps he was the devil himself. She made up her mind to go back to Squire Ekbom and...and what? What would she say? She couldn't tell him about Teo's spear. No matter what she said, he would answer with his malicious laugh. Nor was there any other place Teo could sleep—no place where she would be safe. And on a practical level, she could not be without him.

He looked at her curiously when he came back in, obviously wondering why she was up so early. He shrugged and willingly sat down to an early breakfast before going outside to work.

She began having nightmares centered around his spear: That she was holding it, stroking it, squeezing it, that it was poking at her. Each time she awoke breathless, her lower abdomen thrusting rhythmically back and forth.

Then one Sunday morning, she was awakened by the sound of her own moaning and, her fingers playing between her legs. It was then that she knew the devil had taken possession of her. It was more than she could bear.

She put on her church clothes and taking her Bible from the shelf, hurried along the familiar path to the village. Because she was early, no one was yet in the chapel. Elin took her usual place on the organ bench and struck a loud, violent chord.

"Be gone!" she cried, in an attempt to drive away the devil. The chord was so powerful that the entire organ vibrated, and Elin with it. She screamed in horrified ecstasy, then banged her fists down on the keys, causing one long horrific discordant blast, before running from the building. The devil was at her heels.

"Get away! Leave me alone!" she cried over and over as she ran through the village crazily.

People on their way to chapel stepped aside to let her pass, too frightened by her screaming to stop her. Up on the railroad bridge, a group of men stood waiting to watch the morning freight train pass under them, a Sunday morning tradition. They, too, automatically stepped aside as she ran toward them, obviously possessed. Just as she reached the middle of the bridge, the whistle blew. As if on cue, Elin threw herself head first over the railing onto the passing box cars, breaking her neck.

Afterward, people began to speculate about Teo. Had he perhaps raped her? But when questioned, he wrote a statement saying he had never come anywhere near her. He laid the paper on the Bible, raised his right hand and, looking his interrogator in the eye, shook his head. The autopsy verified his statement. She was still a virgin.

Strangely, it was Squire Ekbom who came closest to the truth.

"She needed a man," he declared in his usual malicious way. "Teo's mere presence attracted her body but contradicted her pious convictions. It wasn't Teo who was the devil; it was she herself."

Or was it he who was the devil?

TORA

The cold January wind swept down the mountainside and across the narrow valley, dumping its load of Arctic snow on the few homesteads scattered just below the tree line. Homesteading in northern Sweden during the first years of the 1900s was a hard life. Unlike pioneering in the New World, where settlers could either kill or drive out the enemy, here they were completely at its mercy. For here it was not human beings but rather the weather that was the unpredictable and uncontrollable enemy, sometimes aiding one's labors with both sun and rain, while other times destroying one's efforts with too much of one or the other. Either way, poverty was never far away. Even in the good years, it stood on the doorstep; in the bad years, it moved inside and made itself an unwelcome guest.

Tora bent over the raised open hearth, stirring porridge in a three-legged iron pot standing in the fire. Outside, the wind howled eerily around the log cabin, rattling the door and demanding to be let in. Here and there, snowflakes managed to force their way between the wall timbers and fell silently to the floor, building small drift-like piles that had no intention of melting in the chilly room. The insides of all three of the cabin's small windows were covered with a thick layer of ice, except for a tiny peep hole one of the smaller children had scraped on one of them out of boredom.

It was already dark even though it was only three o'clock, but the lamp wouldn't be lit for another couple of hours, when it was officially evening. Kerosene was not only expensive, but also difficult to carry home on one's back over the rough mountain paths. In the meantime, the flickering light from the fire sufficed.

Tora pulled her long, baggy sweater more tightly around her thin body with her free hand. The sweater had belonged to her grandmother, who wore it winter and summer. After she died, her mother cut off the too-long sleeves, unraveled them past the holes in the elbows, and sewed them back on again. There must have been buttons on it at one time, for there were button holes down one edge of the front, but they had long since disappeared. Granny had always held it closed with a large safety pin, the only one Tora had ever seen. When she had learned that the sweater was to be hers, the prospect of inheriting that safety pin excited her even more than the sweater itself. But to her dismay, when she finally got it, the pin was gone, replaced by one black button at the neck. Not wanting to seem ungrateful, she had said nothing.

Under the sweater, she wore one of her two dresses, the one her mother had remade by "turning" a hand-me-down dress from a cousin, so that the less-faded inside of the material was on the outside. Over it, she wore a pinafore-type apron made from a worn-out, hand-woven sheet. And underneath, she had on the long winter stockings of scratchy woolen yarn that her mother had spun and knitted. Every winter, the toes were opened and knitted a bit longer and the heels re-darned. The leg sections never wore out, nor did their irritating scratchiness cease.

On the floor by the door stood her brand new shoes side by side, waiting for the next morning when she would wear them for the first time. She was nine years old, and they were the only pair of new shoes she had ever owned—high leather ones with hooks instead of holes for the laces. She dared not even look at them for fear they weren't real. They had been a combination birthday and Christmas present, for after the holidays she was going to go to school in town, a two-day journey from home.

Not only that, she was to make the journey all on her own—she who had never even spent a night away from her family. She felt very grown-up, for not even her older brothers had left home on their own yet. At the same time, mixed with her joy was also anxiety, a fear of the unknown awaiting her.

Up until now, Tora's schooling had been rather sporadic. Since there was no school, or even village, within a day's walk, the young children in the area were taught by an ambulatory teacher who spent several weeks at each homestead, teaching those children who lived within walking distance of wherever he happened to be. In return, he was given room and board.

Once his pupils were able to read and write and manage basic addition and subtraction, they had to move on to a school in a little settlement a several hours' walk away. There they boarded at surrounding farms, only coming home on weekends.

Tora's four older brothers had continued their required education in that manner, and it was assumed that she would follow in their footsteps. But when her turn came, there was no place available for her to board. And thus it was decided that she should be sent to town.

Town. She tried to imagine what it was like. The largest place she had been to was a village where an open market was held twice a year. Its only street was lined on both sides with small wooden shacks with large glassless windows on whose wide sills goods were laid out for sale.

On market days, it was crowded with people going from stand to stand, buying coffee, sugar, salt, flour, and other things they were unable to raise or make themselves. The one time she had been there with her father on a non-market day, the whole place had been devoid of people, the window shutters closed, and the doors padlocked. Surely, town wasn't like that—yet she wasn't at all sure.

"Tora," her mother called from across the room, "stop your daydreaming and stir the porridge before it burns to the pot! Otherwise the burned part will be your portion. There's hardly enough for all of us, as it is. And the rest of you, come to the table now. Your father and brothers will be in any minute."

From the dark corners of the room, small feet approached the table. One after the other they climbed up onto the long bench on the far side: Tora's three younger sisters and two little brothers. One of them pulled open the drawer in the table, scooped out a dozen wooden spoons, and began passing them around. Each of them had a personalized spoon, carved by their father for his or her first birthday. When one finished eating, the spoon was licked off carefully, dried on one's shirt or skirt, and returned to the drawer.

There were stamping thuds on the porch and suddenly the door swung open, sucking in a cloud of snow, followed by her father and older brothers.

"Believe it or not, the wind is starting to die down. It will be calm and clear by morning," her father announced, looking at Tora. She began stirring more vigorously, not sure if she was glad or not.

She helped her mother ladle out the porridge into two large wooden bowls. To her surprise, she was told to fetch the syrup jar, whereupon her mother made an indentation in the middle of the porridge in each of the bowls and filled it with a spoonful of golden syrup. Everyone watched in awe. It was only on very special occasions that they had anything sweet with their evening porridge.

Everyone looked at Tora. It was because she was going away. They began to eat, six of them from each communal bowl, slowly and carefully, trying to get their spoons as close as possible to that delicious center without being accused of coming too near it. No one was allowed to take of the syrup until the soft walls of porridge enclosing it gave way, making it impossible not to.

They chattered and laughed, hunching over the bowls, their shoulders pressed together. The icy chill had left the cabin, and everyone seemed light-hearted, in the midst of the storm. Everyone but Tora, whose lip quivered now and then at the thought of leaving the warmth of her large family.

That night, when they covered the floor with the reindeer hides, that served as both their beds and bedding and on which they slept in pairs, all of the younger children begged to share Tora's with her. Long after everyone else had fallen asleep, she lay awake, surrounded by the small bodies pressed against her under the sheepskin, their light even breathing lulling her gently. As the oldest girl, she had helped with the younger ones all their lives, dressing, feeding, watching, and playing with them while her mother was busy with the spinning and weaving, milking and cheese-making, sewing, washing, and all the many household jobs which kept her constantly occupied. It was almost as though they were her own children, as much a part of her as her arms and legs. She wondered how they were going to get along without her.

The wind had abated completely by the time they awoke in the still-dark morning, and the sky was covered with millions of stars, giving the new snow a slightly bluish tint. It had been arranged that when the postman came on his weekly route, Tora would follow him down to the nearest village, some twenty miles away. He had arrived during the night after everyone had gone to bed and, as all travelers in the wilderness, had come in quietly, spread out his reindeer hide in a corner, and quickly fallen asleep. And now he was on his skis again, ready to set off, with the black leather mail pouch strapped to his back.

Everyone gathered around Tora to help her push her new shoes through the leather toe straps on her homemade skis. She was bundled up in an old woolen coat, with a thick shawl wrapped around her head, neck, and upper body. On her back was a square pack basket made of woven strips of birch bark. In it were her other dress, another warm undershirt, an extra pair of underpants, a clean apron, Granny's sweater, and a nightgown made from her father's old shirt. She didn't understand why she needed such a thing, since she was used to sleeping in her underwear and long stockings, but her mother had been adamant when packing it the previous day.

"You are to sleep in this so that people won't think we are dirt poor," she explained. "The only time you can sleep in your underwear is when your nightgown is being washed. And you needn't say that these are all the clothes you own. Just say that these are all you had room for in your pack. That's not a lie."

And to make sure it was not a lie, her mother had loaded the space that was left with a Bible, a comb, Tora's pencil and eraser, and a little coin purse with a few coins in it with which to pay for her transportation and lodging on the way to school, as well as on her return trip at the end of the term. And now, just before lifting it onto Tora's back, she opened the flap and put in food for the trip—a small round loaf of bread and part of a leg of dried reindeer meat wrapped in a cloth.

"Ask Post-Anders politely if you can use his knife, when you need to cut off some meat," her mother told her.

"My spoon…" she began.

"You don't need that. They have real spoons at the school's boarding house. Maybe even forks and knives, too." She paused and reached into her pocket. "And one more thing," she continued, fumbling with the edge of Tora's shawl. "You shall have this, just in case you need it."

She backed away from her daughter stiffly, reluctant to show the unexpected flood of emotion that had suddenly overtaken her. Before Tora could look down, the small children rushed to fill her place, pulling at Tora's coat and ski poles, crying out for her to pick them up, to stay, to take them with her, to come home soon.

"Are you ready?" Post-Anders called over his shoulder.

Tora couldn't answer.

"Come on, line up!" her father commanded, loosening the youngest boy's grip on her leg. Automatically, all nine of them fell into place according to age, leaving a hole where Tora usually stood. Her father stepped forward and placed his hand on her head. "Make us proud of you," he said simply.

Post-Anders pushed off down the gentle slope, and Tora slid out from under her father's hand and followed in his tracks without looking back. As soon as she knew she was out of sight, her fingers sought the edge of her shawl and turned it over. There was the safety pin.

It was dark by the time they arrived at the little inn that had been their goal. Tora was exhausted. She had never skied so far before. Because Post-Anders was behind schedule, having been slowed by her pace, he knocked on the door without removing his skis. When Widow Blom, the proprietress, appeared, he bid Tora a hasty good-bye and disappeared into the night. For the second time that day, she felt abandoned. Even though she hardly knew him, he had been a familiar part of her life as long as she could remember.

As soon as she had warmed herself by the fire and eaten, Widow Blom took her to one of the upstairs rooms. Tora was horrified; there were four or five beds almost as high as tables sticking out into the otherwise empty room. She had never seen a real bed, let alone slept in one. Nor had she ever slept by herself. She clutched Widow Blom's hand pleadingly, afraid to say anything. She had been brought up to obey adults without arguing.

"Do you sleep on the floor at home?" Widow Blom asked.

Tora nodded.

"With lots of brothers and sisters?"

Tora nodded again. "We're ten," she replied.

Without further questioning, Widow Blom led her down the hall to her own room. In one corner was a large cupboard with a curtain hanging across the front. She pulled the curtain aside to reveal a built-in bed with a high wooden edge to hold the straw-filled bolster in place.

"This bed you won't fall out of," she said cheerfully. Tora's mood lightened at the sight of a bed in a cupboard. Suddenly, she was so tired that she could hardly keep her eyes open. Widow Blom helped her undress and climb up into the bed, then sat beside her until she fell asleep.

Once, in the middle of the night, Tora woke up after a bad dream, not knowing where she was. Just as she began to cry, Widow Blom's arm pulled her close, and she slept again.

The next morning, Tora laid a couple of coins on the table after breakfast to pay for her room and board, as her mother had instructed. Widow Blom slid them back to her.

"Keep them and buy something for yourself in town," she said.

Tora looked up at her curiously, not sure she had heard right.

"If anyone asks you, just say it is a present from Widow Blom. Hurry now, they're waiting for you." She pressed the coins into Tora's hand.

In her excitement, Tora almost forgot to curtsy when she said thank you.

The first leg of that day's journey was made with a farmer who was taking his wife to see a doctor in a village at the far end of the long narrow lake. They put Tora between them in the sleigh, tucked reindeer hides around themselves, and set off over the ice. The sun shone in a cloudless sky, but the wind created by their speed stole all its warmth. By the time they got to the village, Tora was cold clear through. They left her at the little train station where she had an hour to wait for a bus. There, the station master's wife took her into her kitchen and set her in front of the woodstove to thaw out, giving her a bowl of hot soup to speed the process. Just as she finished, there was a rumbling sound and then a toot. Going outside, she hesitated, not quite sure she wanted to ride on such a big bus.

"Climb on board, all those who are going to Vilhelmina!" shouted the driver.

"Come on, little lassie. And don't forget your skis over there," called a voice from behind her. Turning around she saw an old Lapp man dressed in a bright red, blue, and yellow tunic and wearing a hat with a huge pom-pom on the top. She recognized him and his wife; they passed by her house every year on their way up into the mountains to help their two grown sons divide the reindeer herds.

Both of them were tiny, not much taller than she herself, and their weather-beaten skin was brown and wrinkled. She was sure they were at least a hundred years old. She didn't like Lapps. They scared her.

They were so different, living in teepees and tying their babies onto boards and hanging them up high to keep them out of the way. And they wore such strange clothes, especially the men who looked like they had on short skirts and tight leggings. And riding in little boat-like sleds pulled by reindeer, instead of ordinary horse-pulled sleighs. They never said much and when they talked to each other, people couldn't understand what they said. No, she preferred to keep her distance from them.

She handed her skis to the driver to tie onto the top of the bus, then climbed up the steps and sat down in the front seat, with her pack on the other seat to prevent anyone from sitting next to her. She had intended to watch every bit of the way from her front row seat, but they hadn't even reached the next village before she had fallen asleep. Several hours later, the Lapp woman woke her. They were driving along Vilhelmina's main street.

"Do you know where you are going when you get off the bus?" she asked.

"To the school," Tora replied, realizing as she said it that she had no idea where the school was.

"Have you been there before?"

Tora shook her head.

"We can show you. We're going that way," the Lapp man volunteered.

She didn't answer. When the bus stopped, the three of them got off, and the man took her skis from the roof. He and his wife set off down the street on either side of her.

Tora was awestruck by all that she saw. Along the edge of the icy street was a raised walkway so that she didn't have to get her new shoes snowy. And on both sides of the street were real shops that one could walk into, with things she could never imagine lying in their windows. So this was what town was like. She could hardly believe it.

All too soon, they reached the school, with its boarding house beside. The term had begun the previous day, and the children were out for recess when they arrived. Tora tried to thank the Lapp couple for their help, in an effort to escape from them before entering the school grounds, but it was as if they didn't hear her. They took her into the building and to the headmaster's office.

"You must be Tora," he said. "We have been expecting you. And these are your parents, I assume." He held out his hand to the old man.

"No! They're not my parents!" she declared, embarrassed beyond belief. "They just showed me where the school was."

She was almost in tears. How could he think that these old Lapp people were her parents! Lapps were considered by many people to be hardly more than animals. She was no Lapp girl! Such an insult!

There was a sharp knock on the door, and a middle-aged woman in a starched blue dress and white apron entered. Her hair was pulled back into a tight bun.

"Oh, this is the boarders' housemother, Fröken Sträng," the headmaster said.

Tora held out her hand and curtsied slightly, but Fröken Sträng ignored the gesture.

"It's about time you got here," she said. "Say good-bye to your parents now and follow me." She grasped Tora's hand and pulled her away from the Lapp couple. A door closed between them, and it was over.

But it wasn't over. Not one child on the playground had missed Tora's arrival with her, "Lapp parents." Before they had even met her they had something on her that they intended to not let her forget. And the more she would maintain that they had not been her parents and that she was not a Lapp, the more they would taunt her, adding for good measure that she was also a liar. Already her place in the social hierarchy was determined beyond recall.

Tora was the last one up to the nine-year-old girls dormitory after dinner that first night. When she opened the door to the spartan sleeping room, fifteen girls were waiting for her. Iron beds lined both of the long walls, with identical wooden cupboards between them. On each side of the door stood a washstand with an enamel washbowl and pitcher on it and, on the wall beside it, a pegboard from which identical towels hung.

She stepped into the room hesitantly. One of the girls slipped behind her and closed the door. Silently, they advanced on her from all directions until she was encircled by a tight ring of nightgown-clad bodies. She smiled, glad for such a welcome—until she realized they were chanting "Lapp-lassie, Lapp-lassie." Suddenly they looked like a pack of snarling dogs.

"I-I-I'm not a L-Lapp," she stammered. "Those people aren't my parents."

"Liar!" someone yelled. "Lyin' Lapp-lassie!"

"I don't even know those old people. They were on the bus only," she tried to explain.

"Little Lapp-liar! Little Lapp-liar!" sang a couple of the older girls, stepping closer to her.

Tora look around, helplessly. She had always had her brothers to protect and defend her. For the first time in her life, she was completely on her own.

"I'm not a Lapp! And I'm not lying!" she screamed.

The door opened behind her.

"What is all this racket about?" Fröken Sträng demanded angrily.

"I'm not a Lapp!," repeated Tora at the top of her lungs.

"Hush, child!" she snapped. "These girls have lived together in harmony until you came along and began making trouble."

"But they're calling me a Lapp and I'm not!"

"Don't talk back! Get into bed now, all of you," she ordered. "Lights out, and mouths closed."

That night Tora cried herself to sleep. Through her sniffling she could hear small voices whispering, "Crybaby! Little lying Lapp!"

The next day she resolved to never again let herself cry in school. And when her nickname became Lill-Lapp[1] she withdrew behind a wall of indifference until she no longer heard their jeering.

Although, to outsiders' eyes, Fröken Sträng gave the appearance of being a substitute mother for those young girls who were away from home for the first time, she had a darker side which manifested itself in a sadistic manner.

One of her standard rules was that, in spite of the fact that there was an indoor toilet, no one was allowed to use it. Instead, they were forced to go out to an outhouse in the corner of the school yard. Even at night.

As if that weren't enough, they were only permitted to go one at a time. As a concession, they could take along a small kerosene lantern, but only on moonless nights. But for many of the girls, the shadows caused by the lantern light were almost as frightening as the darkness.

1 Lill translates into little.

Her method of punishing a wrong-doer was to tell her, "I'll see you in my room tonight at bedtime," leaving the offender to spend the day in anticipation. When bedtime came, everyone in the dormitory had to gather to witness the punishment. The girl was laid across the housemother's lap, her nightgown pulled up, and she was beaten on her bare buttocks with a short-handled broom.

The extent of the beating was not determined by the misdemeanor, but rather, by how long it took Fröken Sträng to work herself into a frenzy.

The first time Tora was forced to witness such a scene, she was so upset that she ran directly up to bed as soon as she could escape from the room, without even going to the toilet or washing her face and hands. Consequently, she dreamed that she was sitting in the outhouse, only to be awakened by wet sheets clinging to her legs. Terrified, she lay wide awake without moving for the rest of the night.

At 5:30 the next morning Fröken Sträng opened the double doors to the dormitory and clicked on the light.

"Everybody up!" she declared, clapping her hands.

All the girls stepped straight out of their sleep onto the floor beside their beds. Except for Tora.

"And what's wrong with Tora?" Fröken Sträng asked harshly, coming towards her.

"I don't feel well, Fröken," she answered.

Fröken Sträng stopped at the foot of the bed and sniffed the air like a horse. Without warning, she flung back the covers.

"Tora doesn't feel well," she mocked. "Well, you're about to feel worse. Get the switch!" she ordered the nearest girl.

Yanking Tora out of bed by the arm, she pulled her wet nightgown over her head, bent her over the edge of the bed, pressing her face into the wet sheet, and whipped her until the quickly raised welts began to bleed. For Tora, who had never in her life even been slapped, the shock and humiliation were as great as the pain. Her

2 Torr translates into dry.

only consolation was that she had managed not to cry.

That was the first of many beatings, for the more Tora worried about wetting the bed, the more it happened. Nor did the others let her forget it. The first thing she heard when she woke up each morning was someone calling out, "Is Tora torr²?" while the others all laughed. Not one of them dared to befriend the girl from the mountains. To them, she was only a lowly little Lapp girl trying to pass herself off as one of them. And a liar. The only attention they gave her was to tease her unmercifully.

So overpowering was Tora's misery that she was unable to separate herself from it. No other reality existed beyond the fear of wetting the bed, being beaten by Fröken Sträng, and the eternal teasing by the other girls. To let herself think of home and her family was too painful to endure. Yet without realizing it, she was careful to keep her mother's safety pin pinned to whatever she was wearing, fingering it unconsciously when she felt most miserable. But even though they were required to write home once a month, she never considered telling her parents what her life was really like. They had sacrificed in order to send her to school, and she must not complain.

Then one day, just when she was on the verge of succumbing to tears, an invisible being seemed to spring out of her and place herself between Tora and the group of jeering girls, much in the same way her older brothers used to defend her. She called herself Tilda.

From that day onward, she hid behind Tilda and let her take the brunt of the teasing, as well as the blame and punishment for her wet bed. With Tilda to protect her and absorb the pain, Tora lived like a clam, enclosed in her shell and unaware of what was going on around her. She neither heard nor spoke. The only thing she cared about was doing well in school, to make her parents proud of her.

For every day that passed, the sun climbed higher in the sky and bit by bit the world began to thaw. The snow in the streets turned to slush, then gathered into puddles which in turn overflowed into little rivulets, which ran toward the lake bordering the town. The first tiny wildflowers struggled to push aside last autumn's soggy leaves so they could dance in the mild winds from the south. Then one day, the air was filled with birdsong, and spring had arrived.

Tora began to anticipate the end of the school term when she could finally go home. May came and went, but she hardly noticed. Her life's clock was set for the end of the first week in June, when she would be free from the nightmare of the past months. As that day drew nearer, her mood lightened. Now and again she could let herself think about her family at home without tears coming. Along with everyone else, she began gathering together her few belongings.

The evening before the end of term ceremonies, she was called in to Fröken Sträng's office. Wistfully, she presented herself, wondering what she had done wrong this time.

"You needn't have all your things packed by tomorrow," Fröken Sträng said. "You won't be going home until next week."

For the first time in months, someone's words penetrated her protective wall. Her eyes flared in anger. Although she said nothing, her look caused Fröken Sträng to explain defensively.

"I need help with all the washing and ironing and mending of bedding and cleaning of the dormitory rooms," she answered. "I've already written your mother and informed her that you will be home a week later than expected."

"Why me?" Tora screamed. "I want to go home!"

"Watch your mouth, young lady! It's already arranged."

Tora bit her lip to keep from crying as she stalked out of the housemother's office. Her fingers sought the safety pin fastened on the inside of her sweater pocket, opening and closing it over and over in her anger. This time Tilda had failed to come to her rescue.

The following day, the sky was a deep, cloudless blue and the air warm and summery. Everyone in the dormitory dressed in their finest clothes in preparation for the end-of-term ceremonies. The auditorium was decorated with birch branches whose first tiny leaves were just beginning to uncurl, giving off a delicious aroma. Everyone was in the highest of spirits—except for Tora. She put on the same dress she had worn for the last two weeks and didn't bother to re-braid her hair.

Once everyone was seated below the stage, with the headmaster, Fröken Sträng, and all the teachers looking down on them, Tilda took over, and Tora disappeared into herself completely. She never heard her name called out as the student in her class with the highest marks. One of the other girls poked her in the ribs to get her attention.

"Leave me alone!" Tilda screamed, slapping away the girl's hand.

Refusing to go up onto the stage to accept her award, Tora continued to sit with her arms crossed over her chest, staring vacantly into space. What should have been one of the proudest days of her young life was, instead, a day filled with hate and anger.

Afterward, while the students and their parents were having refreshments, she hid in the cellar of the boarding house, the only place where she couldn't hear the voices of the girls calling good-bye to each other as they left with their families. She longed to leave with them, to run away, but there was nowhere for her to go, no way for her to get home now. The bus that connected with the weekly boat had already gone.

During the week that followed, Tora and Fröken Sträng worked side-by-side, first washing and rinsing by hand the sheets from the forty beds in the entire dormitory, hanging them up to dry, then cranking them through the huge mangle, and finally folding them into fourths and rolling them like fat sausages before putting them away in the storage cupboard.

The same process was repeated with the pillow cases, but with one added procedure. Each one had three pairs of ties to keep the pillow from gliding out of the case. Not only must they be folded so that the ties all hung down over the edge of the pile when they were stacked in the cupboard, but the ties must all be crinkled with a gadget resembling a pair of scissors. Since there was only one of these devices, the task was left to Tora, with Fröken Sträng checking from time to time to make sure she was doing it properly. Any that didn't meet her approval were pulled out, often in such a way that the whole pile had to be restacked and arranged. Then the sleeping rooms had to be scrubbed from ceiling to floor, and the large windows washed.

Whatever Fröken Sträng's intention was in choosing Tora to help her—punishment, dislike, curiosity, sadistic pleasure—she failed to make any sort of contact with her whatsoever. Tora's eyes were glazed over and vacant, and she responded to instructions mechanically. She never spoke, nor did the sharpest reprimand cause any reaction. She no longer even needed Tilda to hide behind. Nothing could touch her. At the end of the week, even though the cleaning was not finished, she took her pack basket with her few belongings, put her skis over her shoulder, and disappeared through the gate of the school yard.

This time, when she made her way through the town, no one hurried her along. She had over an hour before the bus left. At the bottom of her apron pocket jingled the two coins Widow Blom had returned to her that long-ago morning. She had never had a chance to spend them, since school girls were not allowed to go into town. Nor had there been anything particular that she wanted.

But now as she examined each shop window she passed, she was amazed at all the things there were to want. It was impossible to choose just one thing. And then suddenly she saw it—a sewing kit with pins and needles, a thimble, four small spools of different colored thread, and even a tiny pair of scissors, in a little cloth-covered box that was held closed with a snap. Never had she seen anything so grand! It was exactly what her mother needed!

But as she stared more closely at it, she realized that it, of course, cost more than the fifty öre in her pocket. Sighing, she backed away from the window to continue down the street.

"Come in and look at it," a voice called to her.

She had been so absorbed in the sewing kit that she hadn't noticed the clerk standing in the open doorway taking the breeze.

Tora obeyed like a robot.

The woman leaned over the low curtain at the back edge of the display window, picked up the sewing kit, blew a bit of dust off it, and handed it to her.

"Are you on your way home from boarding school?" she asked.

Tora nodded.

"Do you have far to go?"

"To Fatmomakke," she answered absently.

"Oh, you have a long journey ahead of you."

All the while, Tora's small fingers ran gently back and forth over the contents of the sewing kit in the same way a blind person would "look" at a fragile bird's egg. Finally, she closed the lid, snapped it, and turned the box over. The price was written on the bottom: fifty-five öre. She set it on the counter and started toward the door.

"Wait a minute!" the saleswoman called. "How much money do you have?"

Tora dug in her pocket and pulled out the two twenty-five öre coins.

"Give them to me," she said kindly.

Tora placed them on the counter obediently, while the woman tore off a piece of brown paper from the roll at the end of the counter and set about wrapping the sewing kit. Lastly, she tied a red ribbon around it.

"You can use this for a hair ribbon," she said, sliding it across the counter. "You have a good trip now."

Tora curtsied. "Thank you, ma'am," she said shyly. Her heart was thumping so wildly that she was sure the woman could hear it.

At last she was on her way home! The June sun, that barely dipped below the horizon during the daylight nights, had finally melted the last of the ice on Lake Malgomaj, and the ferry was running again. Just buying a ticket and walking the gangplank all by herself made Tora feel grown up, not to mention being able to sit out on the open deck without any adult to tell her to be careful.

As the ferry made its way northward, she felt as though she was waking up from a long sleep. Voices penetrated her wall of silence, and she became aware of the people around her. Nor did she find them threatening, like the people at school. All at once, she was overcome with an intense longing for her family—a longing which she had refused to let herself feel during the never-ending nightmare of school. Now she felt like she would burst into tears if she didn't get home soon.

"Oh, hello there!" Widow Blom cried when Tora appeared in the doorway of the inn. "Come in, come in. How was school?"

Tora was completely taken aback. She had long ago made up her mind that she was never going to tell anyone what it had been like. It had never occurred to her that people might ask.

"It was fine," she lied to avoid remembering.

"Your parents will certainly be glad to see you."

"I bought something for my mother with the money you gave back to me," Tora offered quickly, seeing a chance to change the subject.

"Oh, what?"

"Do you want to see it?"

"If you want to show it to me."

She pulled things out of her pack basket until she came to the package. Carefully, she unwrapped it, so as not to destroy the paper.

"Do you think she will like it?" she asked, holding up the sewing kit.

"She will love it," Widow Blom assured her.

"I hope so. She only has one needle and some black thread, and no scissors or thimble." It was the first normal conversation she had carried on in months.

While they admired it, Tora unpinned the safety pin from her dress and laid it inside the sewing kit beside the needles. Then she replaced the wrapping paper, and Widow Blom retied the ribbon while she pressed her finger on the knot.

"What is this?" Widow Blom asked, picking up a paper that had fallen on the floor from among Tora's things. "Your report card?"

Tora nodded.

"May I look at it?"

She shrugged.

Widow Blom's eyes grew big when she opened it. "All A's!" she exclaimed. "Oh, Tora, your parents are going to be so proud of you! Congratulations!"

In that instant Tora understood that showing her report card would put an end to any questions about school.

"I can sleep in one of those regular beds now," Tora said on the way upstairs after supper.

"It's pretty lonely in this big room all by oneself," Widow Blom remarked when they came to the door of the big sleeping room. "You're more than welcome to sleep in my bed again, if you wish. I thought it was nice and cozy last time."

Tora gladly accepted her offer. Widow Blom's presence made her feel secure in a way she hadn't felt since the first night she slept there. And she knew she would never wet the bed.

Then next morning, Post-Anders was eating breakfast in the kitchen of the inn when Tora came downstairs.

"Well, here's the pupil from the big town!" he declared. "I hear you did all right by yourself. Congratulations!"

Now that there was no snow, Post-Anders was able to do his postal route with a horse and two-wheeled cart. In several hours, Tora was home. He pulled to a stop by the outer gate and handed her the weekly newspaper, which was the only mail for her father that day.

"You run along now and show that report card to your parents," Post-Anders told her.

She jumped to the ground, and he handed down her pack basket. She had barely gotten the gate closed behind her before she dropped her things and ran up the uneven path as fast as she could.

"Mamma! Mamma!" she yelled. "Mamma!"

The front door opened, and she threw herself in her mother's arms.

"Little Tora, whatever is the matter? Are you OK?"

"Oh Mamma, it was awful! People were so cruel..." She could no longer hold back her tears, nor her resolve not to tell how she had been treated. The nightmare of the past five months exploded from inside of her in one long torrent, horrifying her parents.

Tora's report card was framed and hung on the wall under the picture of the Royal Family, and she never went back to boarding school in Vilhelmina.

www.ingramcontent.com/pod-product-compliance
Lightning Source LLC
Chambersburg PA
CBHW060455260626
47161CB00005B/2115